SUPER NARWHAL AND JELLY JOLT

BEN CLANTON

tundra

FOR THEO!
MY SUPER SON!

Text and illustrations copyright © 2017 by Ben Clanton
This paperback edition published by Tundra Books, 2018

Tundra Books, an imprint of Penguin Random House Canada Young Readers, a Penguin Random House Company

Library and Archives Canada Cataloguing in Publication

Clanton, Ben, 1988-, author, illustrator
Super Narwhal and Jelly Jolt / Ben Clanton.

(A Narwhal and Jelly book)
Issued in print and electronic formats.
ISBN 978-1-101-91919-4 (paperback). —ISBN 978-1-101-91830-2 (epub)

I. Graphic novels. I. Title.

PZ7.7.C53Sup 2017   j741.5'973   C2016-905226-5
                                                   C2016-905227-3

Published simultaneously in the United States of America by Tundra Books of Northern New York,
an imprint of Penguin Random House Canada Young Readers, a Penguin Random House Company

Library of Congress Control Number: 2016948348

Edited by Tara Walker and Jessica Burgess
Designed by Ben Clanton and Andrew Roberts
The super-duper artwork in this book was rendered in colored pencil, watercolor, ink and colored digitally.
The text was handlettered by Ben Clanton.

Photos: (waffle) © Tiger Images/Shutterstock; (strawberry) © Valentina Razumova/Shutterstock;
(pickle) © dominitsky/Shutterstock; (tuba) Internet Archive Book Images

Printed and bound in China

www.penguinrandomhouse.ca

6 7 8   22 21 20 19

Penguin
Random House
tundra | TUNDRA BOOKS

CONTENTS

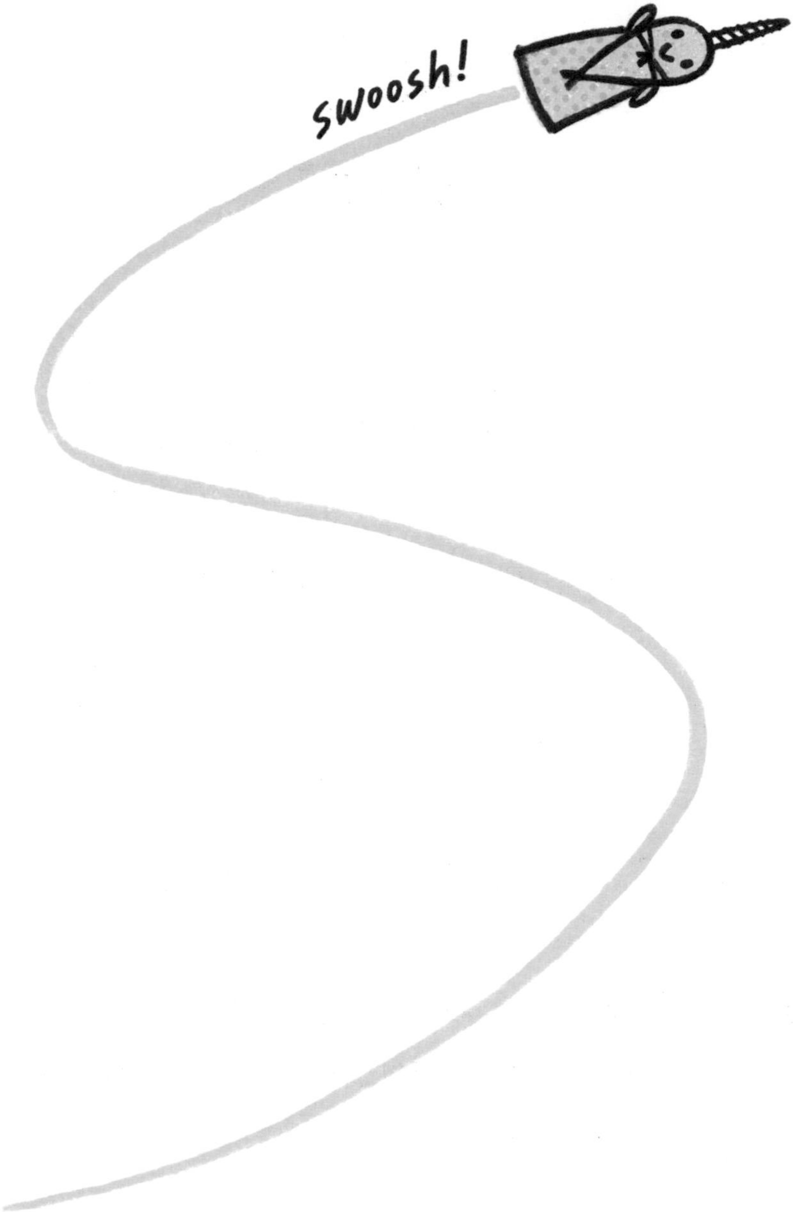
swoosh!

A SUPER START!

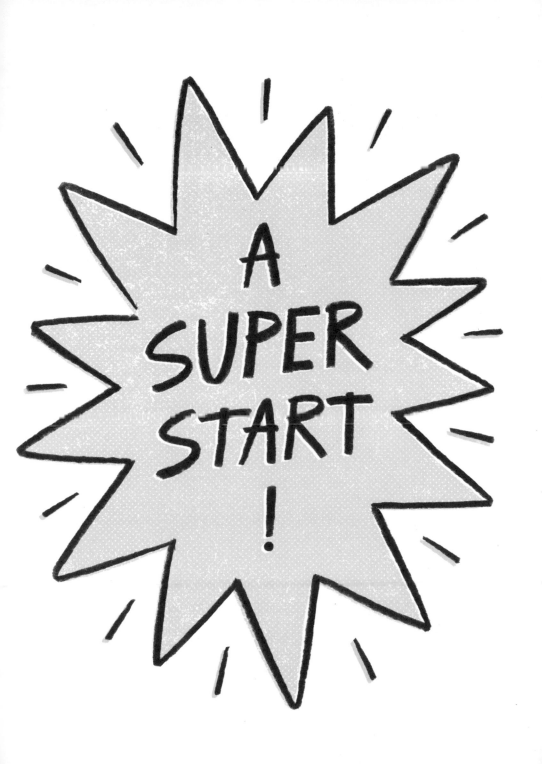

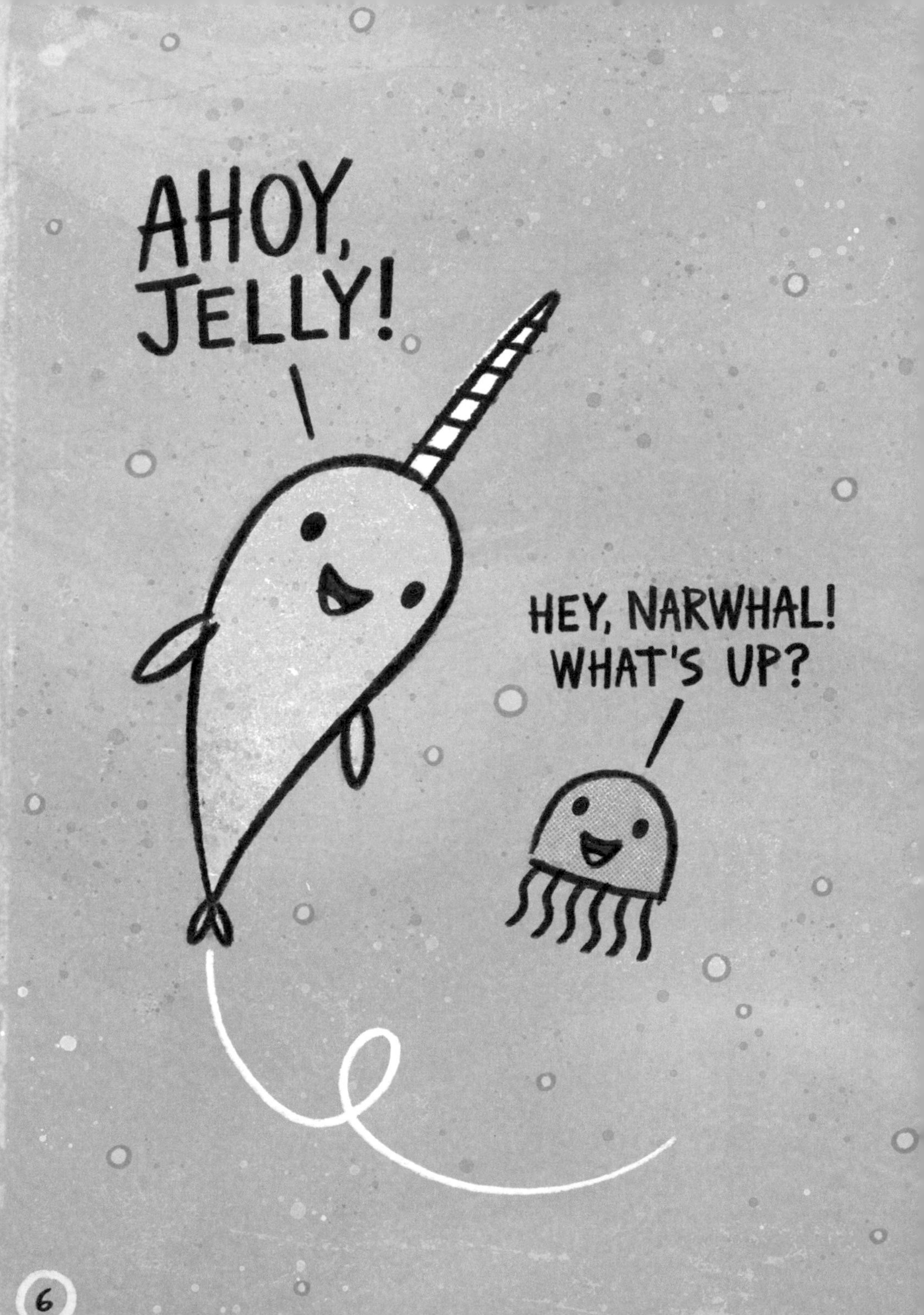
AHOY, JELLY!
HEY, NARWHAL! WHAT'S UP?

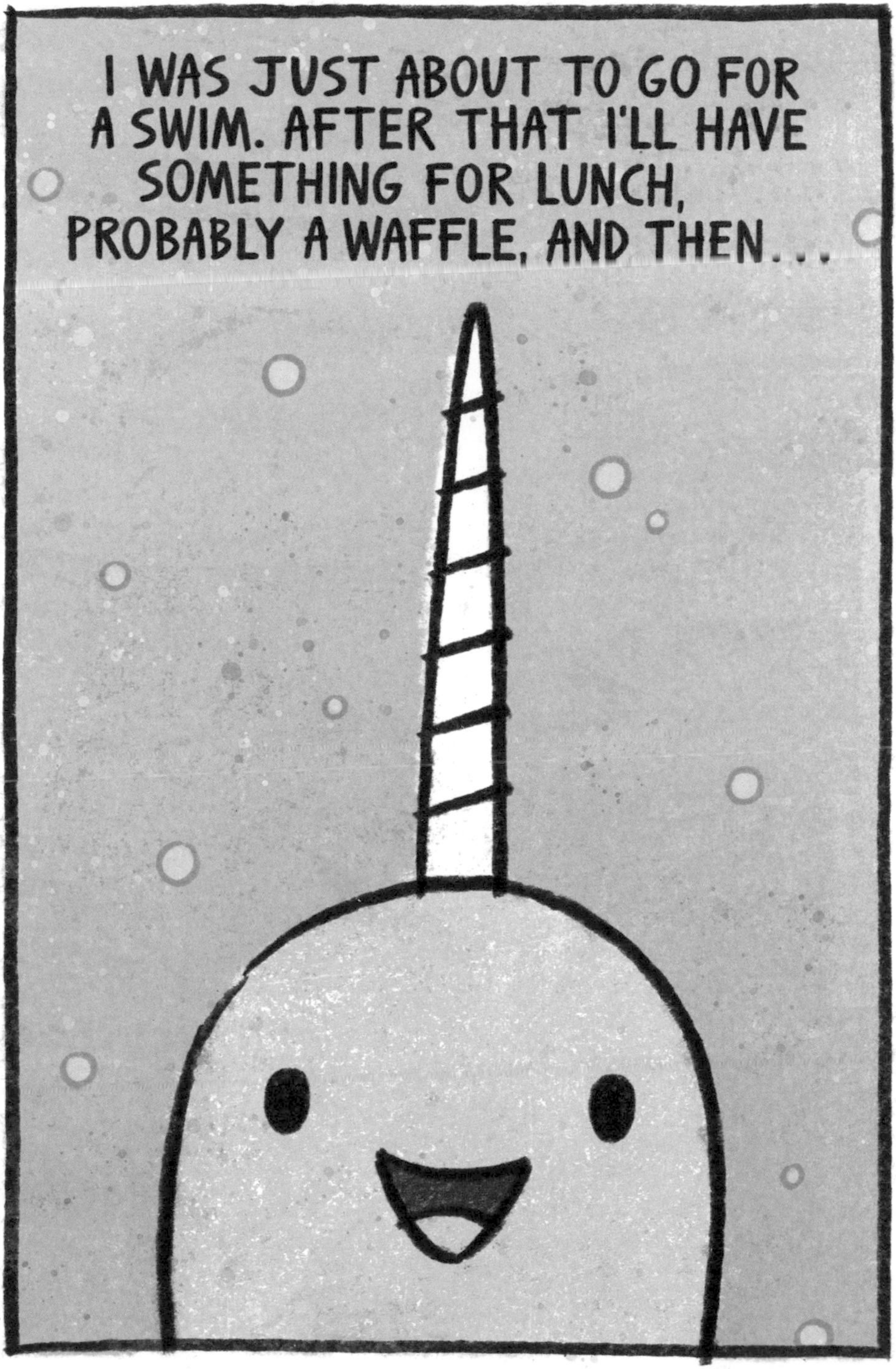
I WAS JUST ABOUT TO GO FOR A SWIM. AFTER THAT I'LL HAVE SOMETHING FOR LUNCH, PROBABLY A WAFFLE, AND THEN . . .

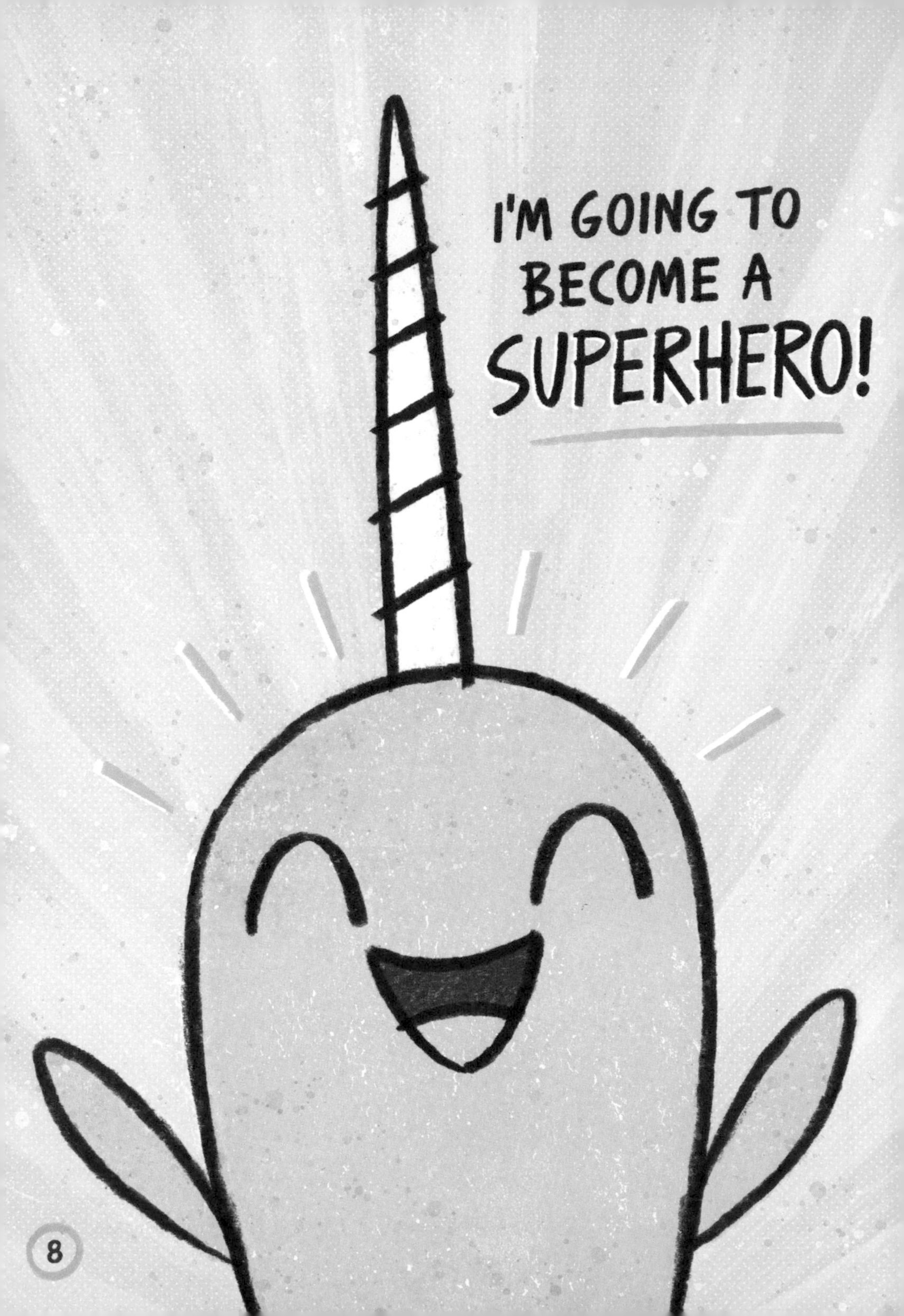
I'M GOING TO BECOME A SUPERHERO!

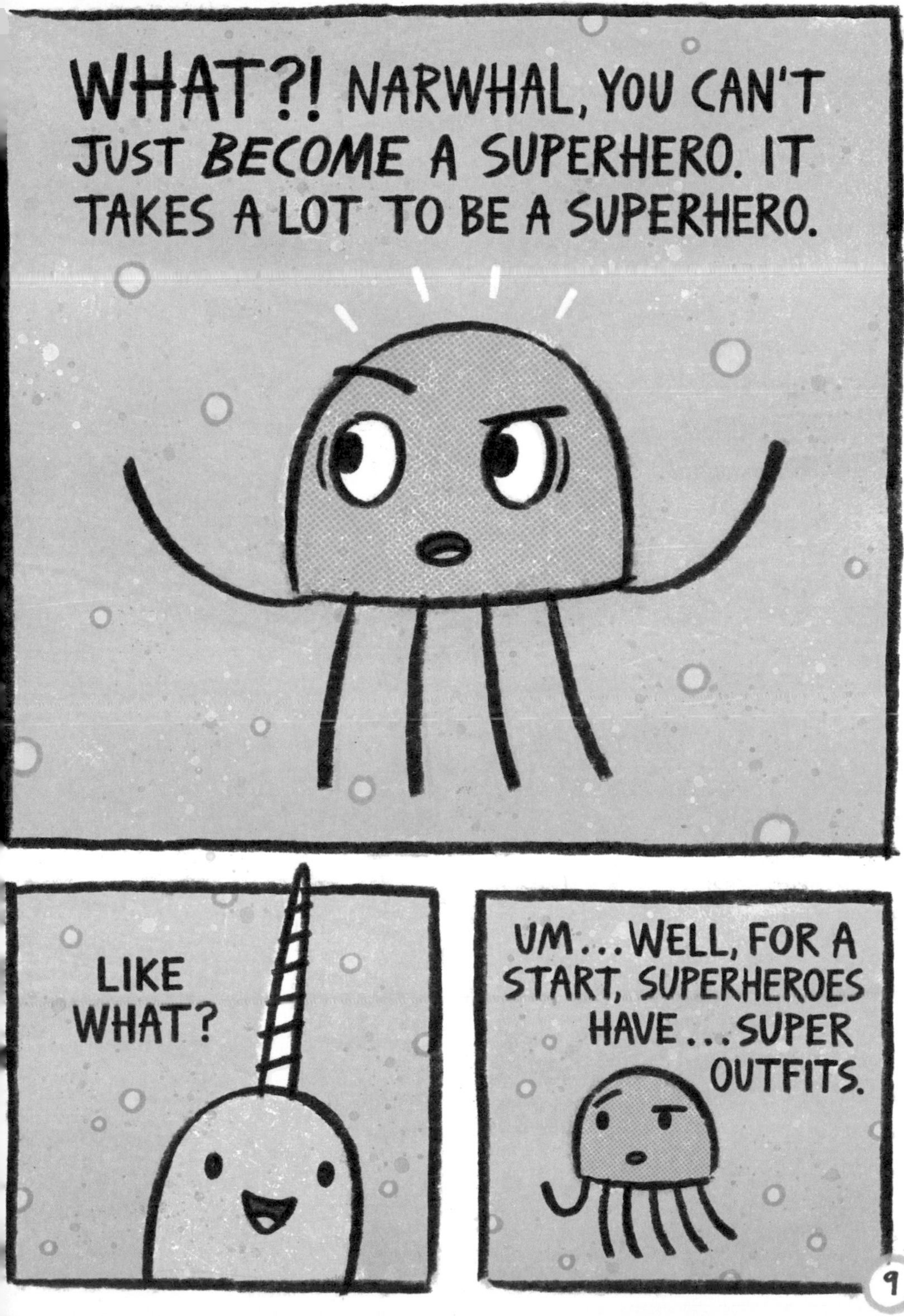
WHAT?! NARWHAL, YOU CAN'T JUST *BECOME* A SUPERHERO. IT TAKES A LOT TO BE A SUPERHERO.
LIKE WHAT?
UM...WELL, FOR A START, SUPERHEROES HAVE...SUPER OUTFITS.

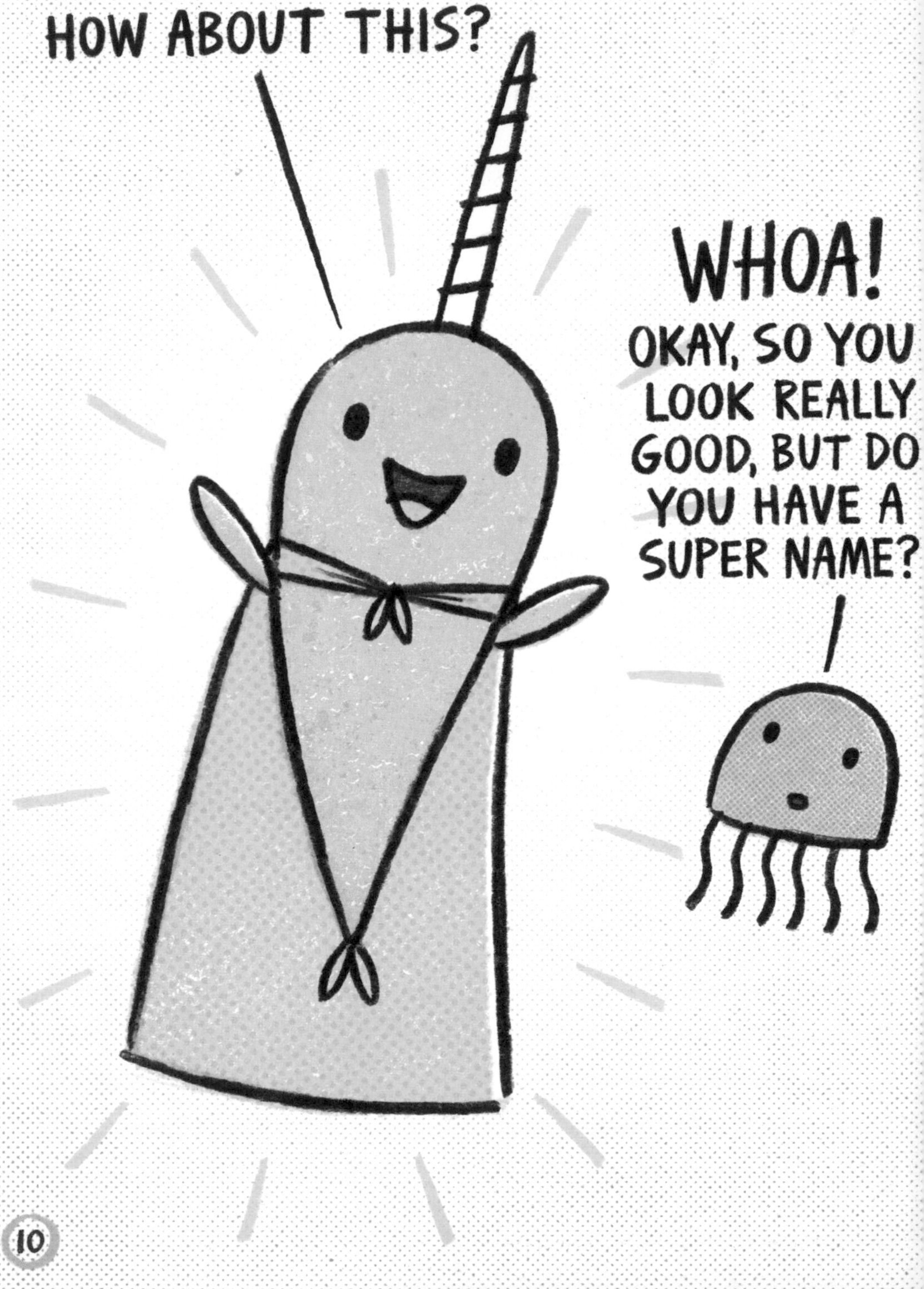
HOW ABOUT THIS?
WHOA!
OKAY, SO YOU LOOK REALLY GOOD, BUT DO YOU HAVE A SUPER NAME?

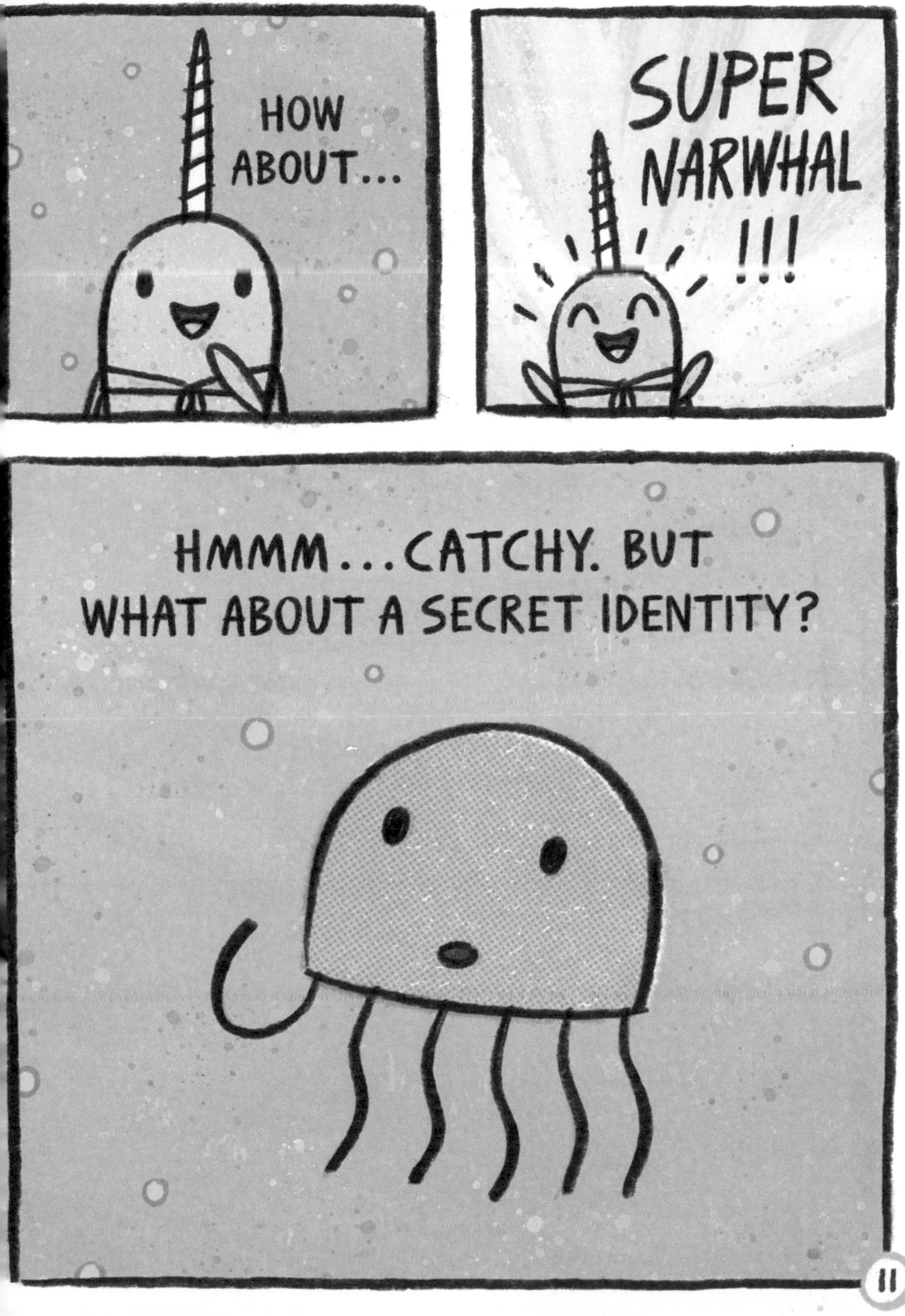
HOW ABOUT...
SUPER NARWHAL !!!
HMMM...CATCHY. BUT WHAT ABOUT A SECRET IDENTITY?

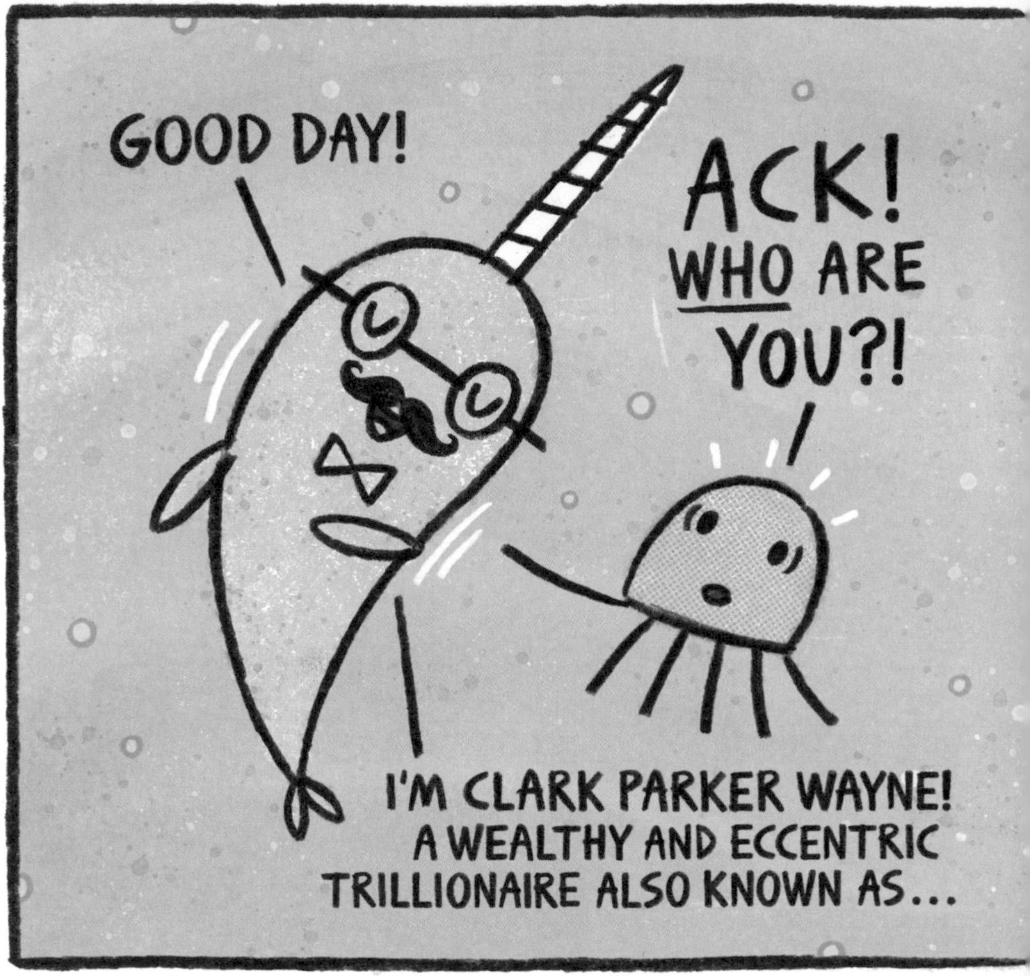
GOOD DAY!
ACK! WHO ARE YOU?!
I'M CLARK PARKER WAYNE! A WEALTHY AND ECCENTRIC TRILLIONAIRE ALSO KNOWN AS...

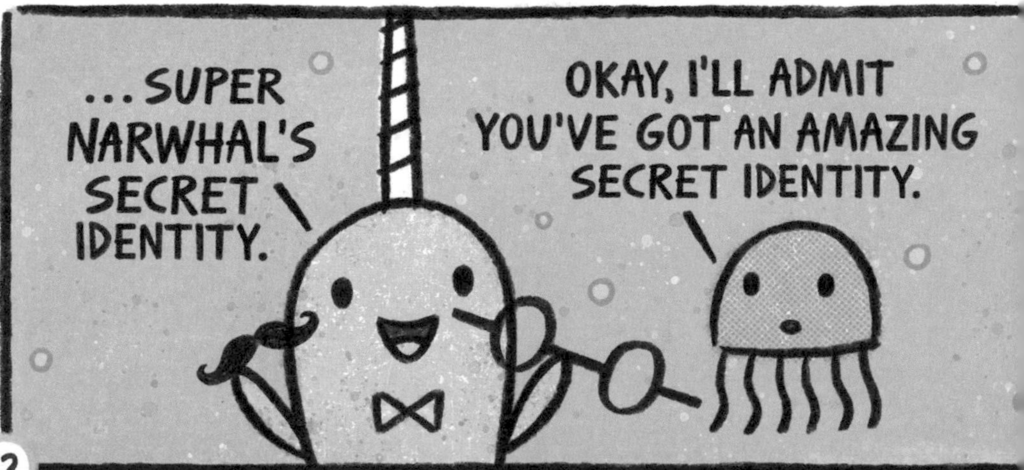
...SUPER NARWHAL'S SECRET IDENTITY.
OKAY, I'LL ADMIT YOU'VE GOT AN AMAZING SECRET IDENTITY.

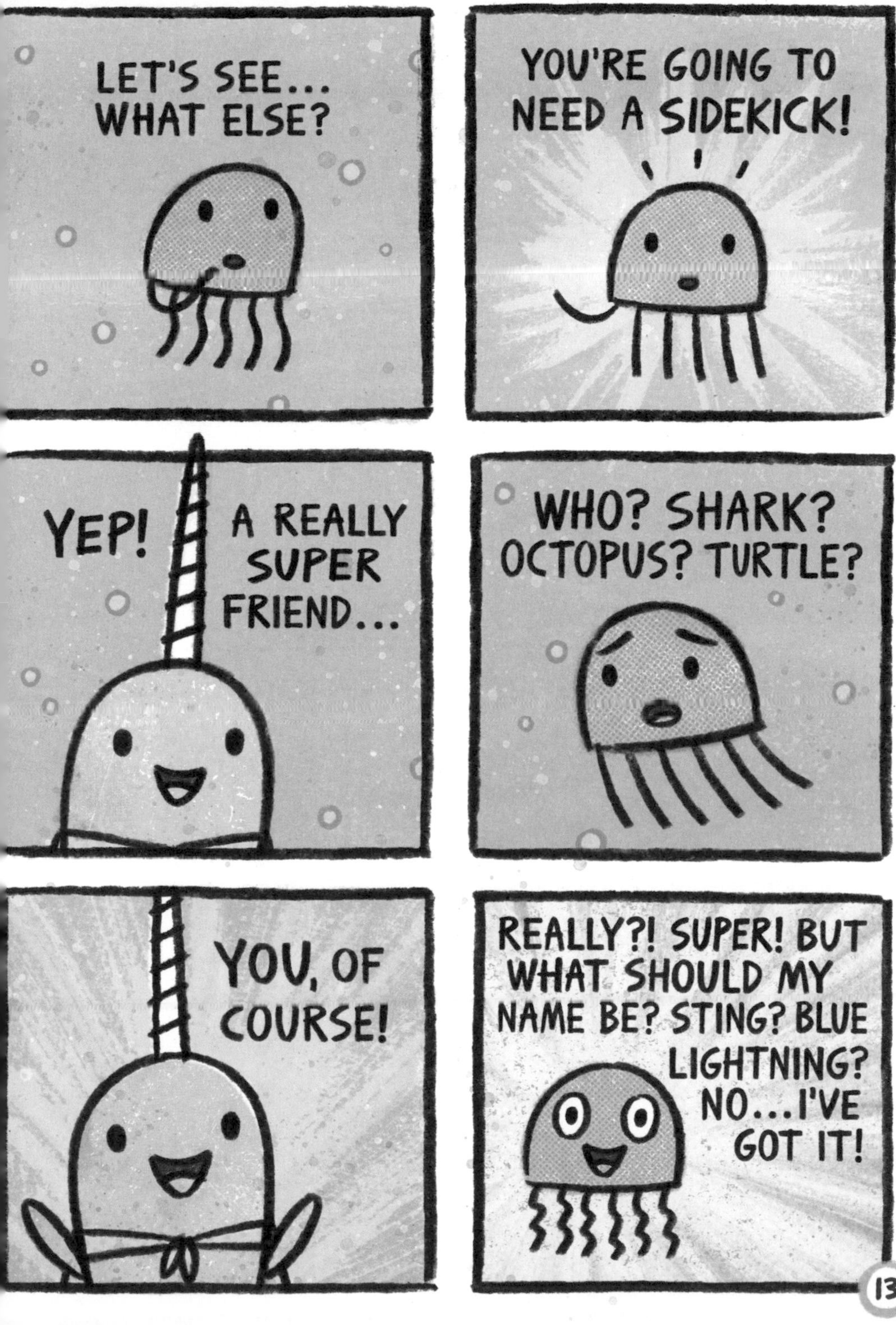
LET'S SEE... WHAT ELSE?
YOU'RE GOING TO NEED A SIDEKICK!
YEP!
A REALLY SUPER FRIEND...
WHO? SHARK? OCTOPUS? TURTLE?
YOU, OF COURSE!
REALLY?! SUPER! BUT WHAT SHOULD MY NAME BE? STING? BLUE LIGHTNING? NO...I'VE GOT IT!

JELLY JOLT THE SUPER SIDEKICK!

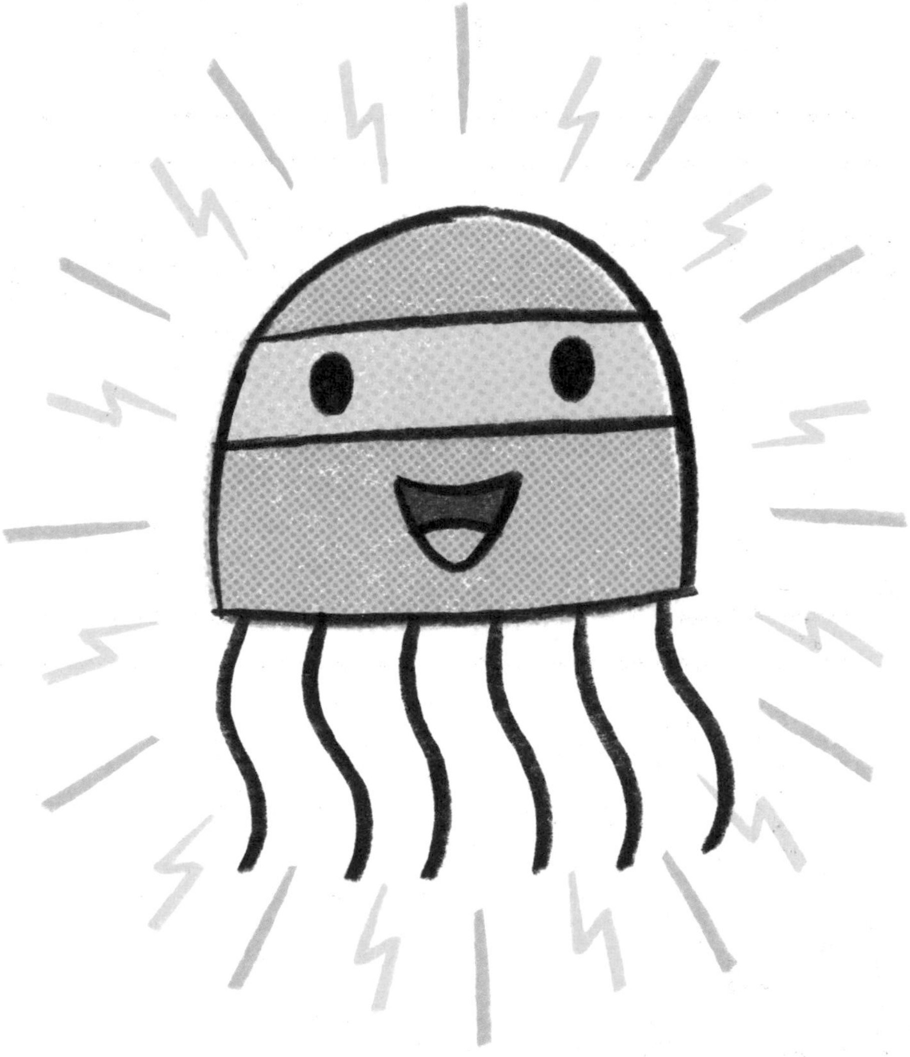

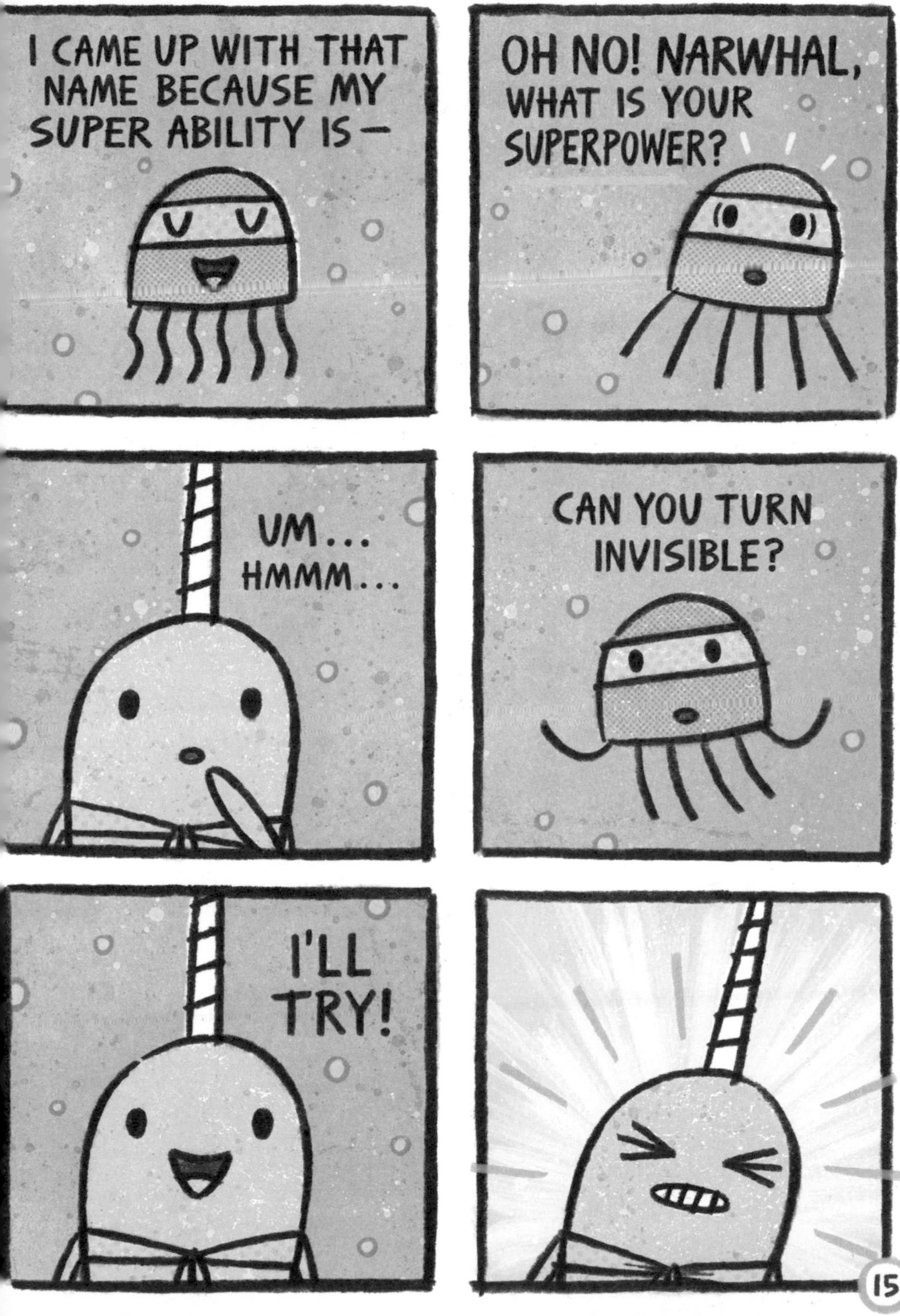
I CAME UP WITH THAT NAME BECAUSE MY SUPER ABILITY IS—
OH NO! NARWHAL, WHAT IS YOUR SUPERPOWER?
UM... HMMM...
CAN YOU TURN INVISIBLE?
I'LL TRY!

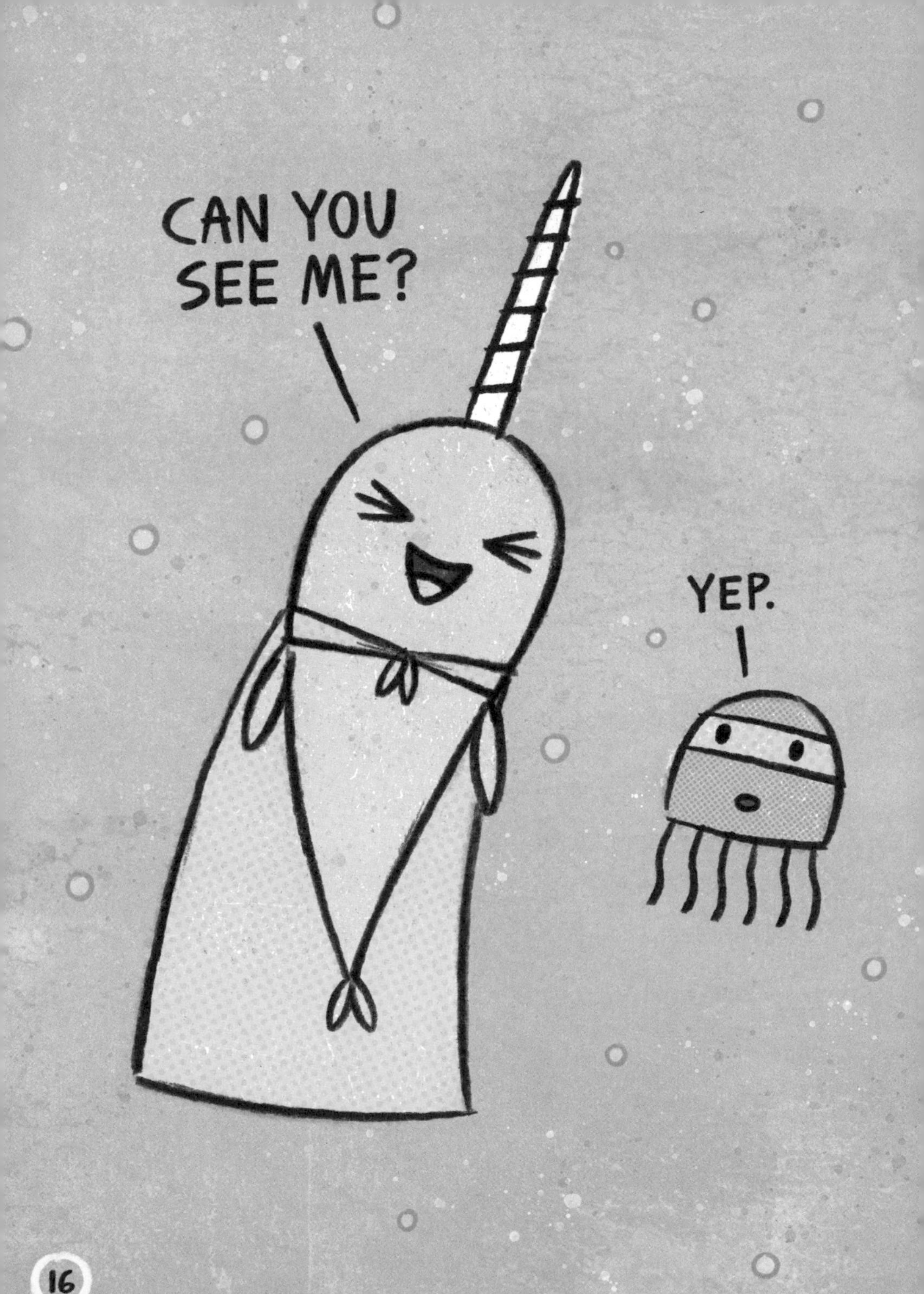
CAN YOU SEE ME?
YEP.

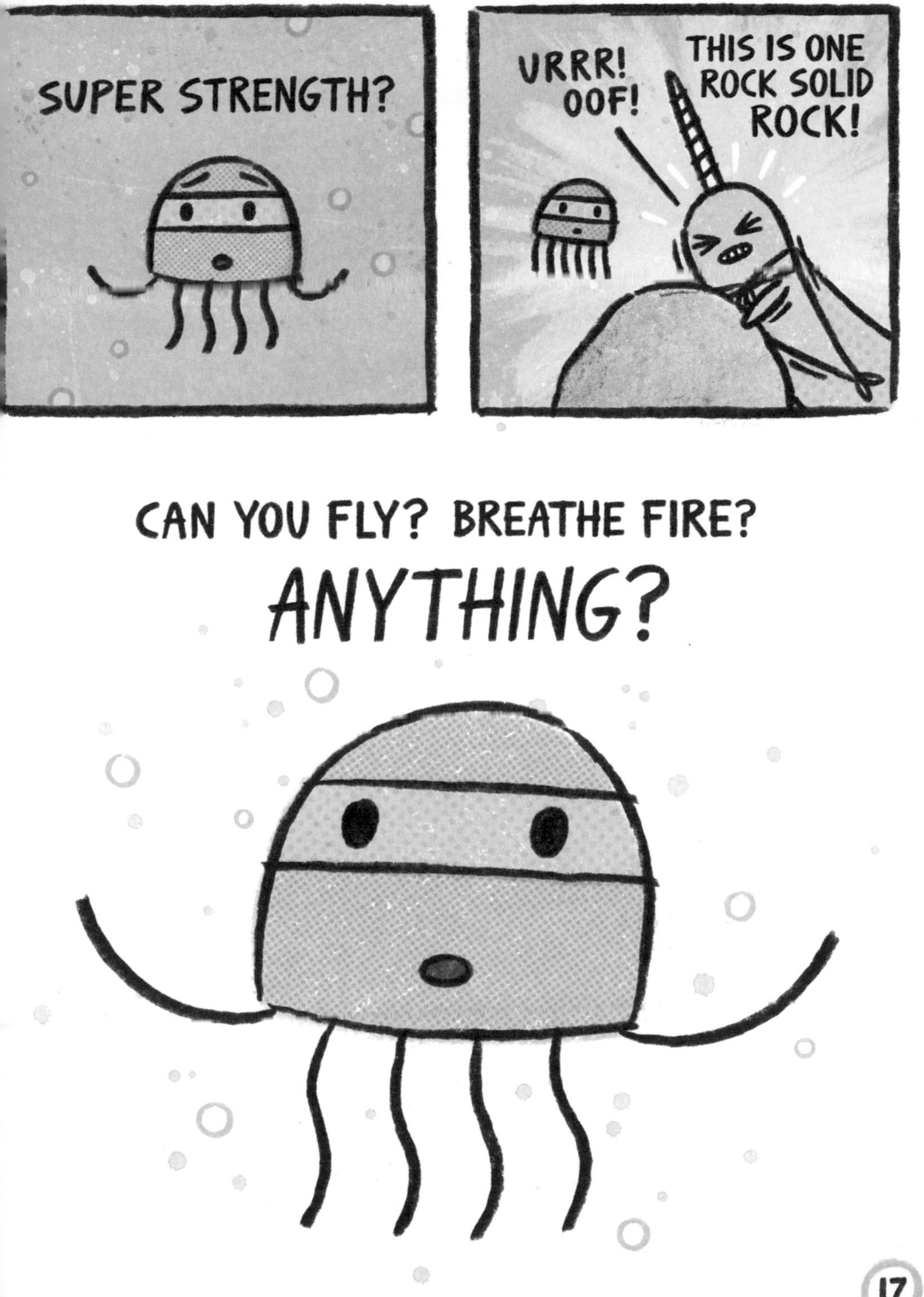
SUPER STRENGTH?
URRR! OOF!
THIS IS ONE ROCK SOLID ROCK!
CAN YOU FLY? BREATHE FIRE?
ANYTHING?

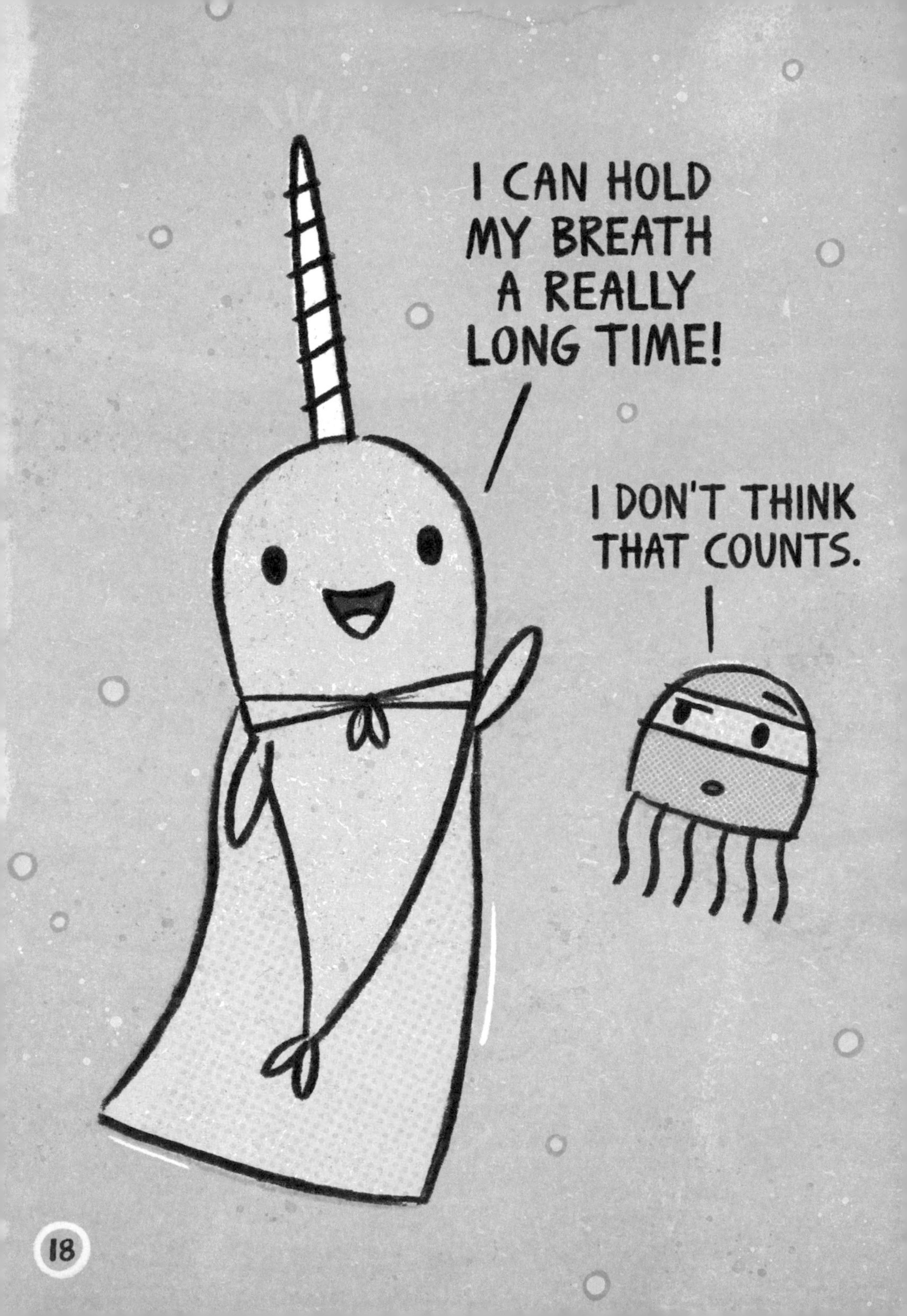

I CAN HOLD MY BREATH A REALLY LONG TIME!
I DON'T THINK THAT COUNTS.

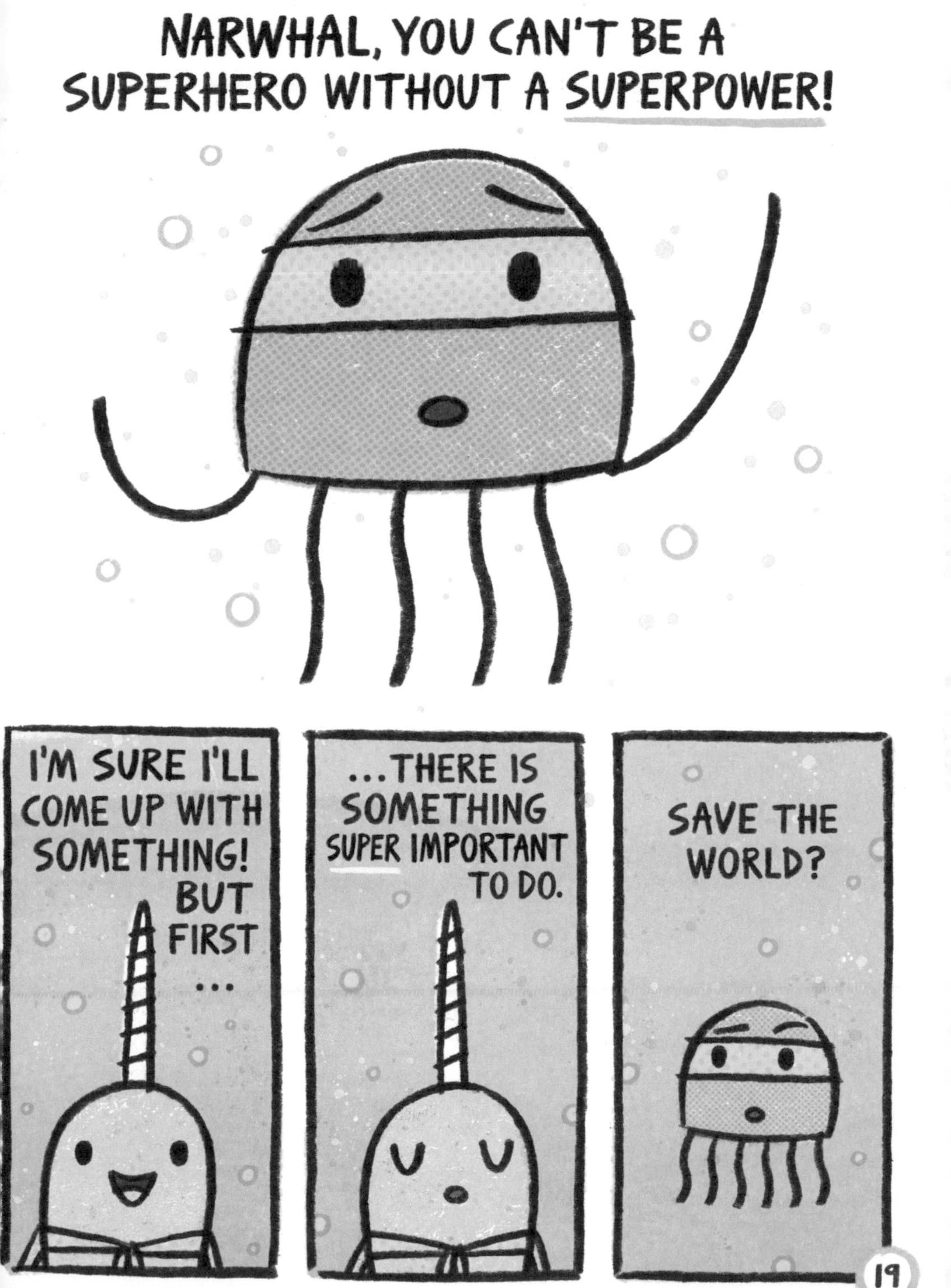
NARWHAL, YOU CAN'T BE A SUPERHERO WITHOUT A SUPERPOWER!
I'M SURE I'LL COME UP WITH SOMETHING!
BUT FIRST ...
...THERE IS SOMETHING SUPER IMPORTANT TO DO.
SAVE THE WORLD?

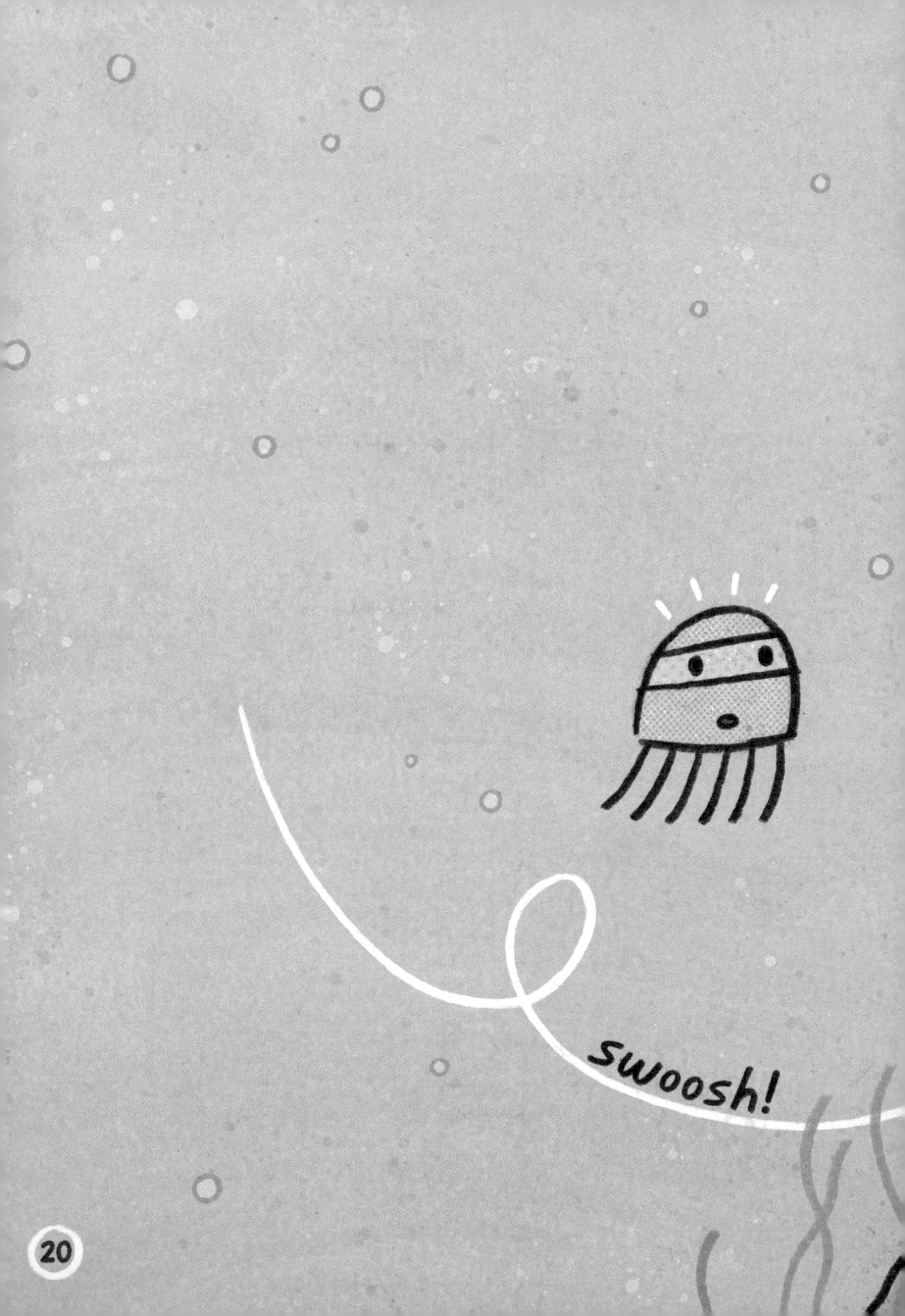
swoosh!

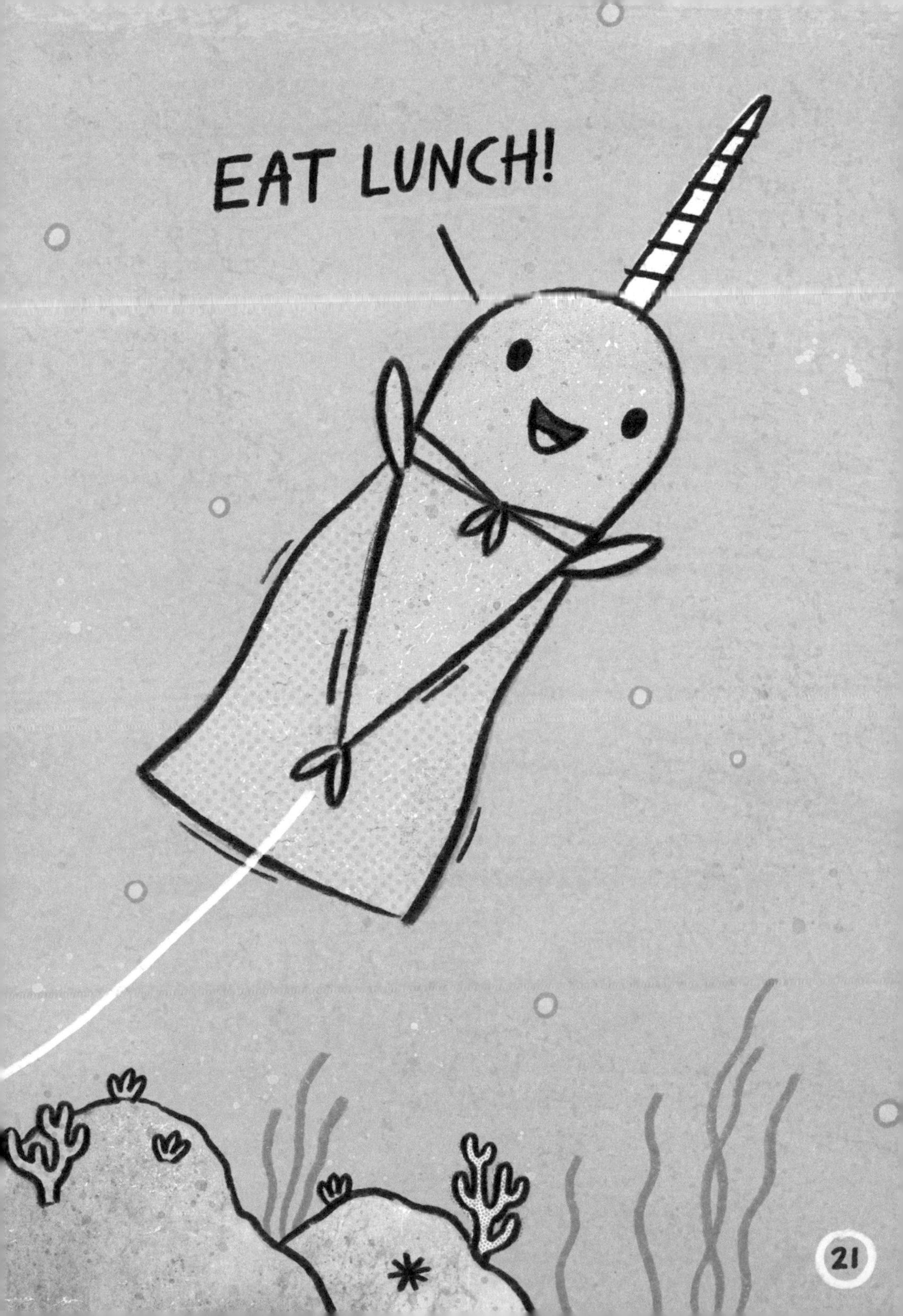
EAT LUNCH!

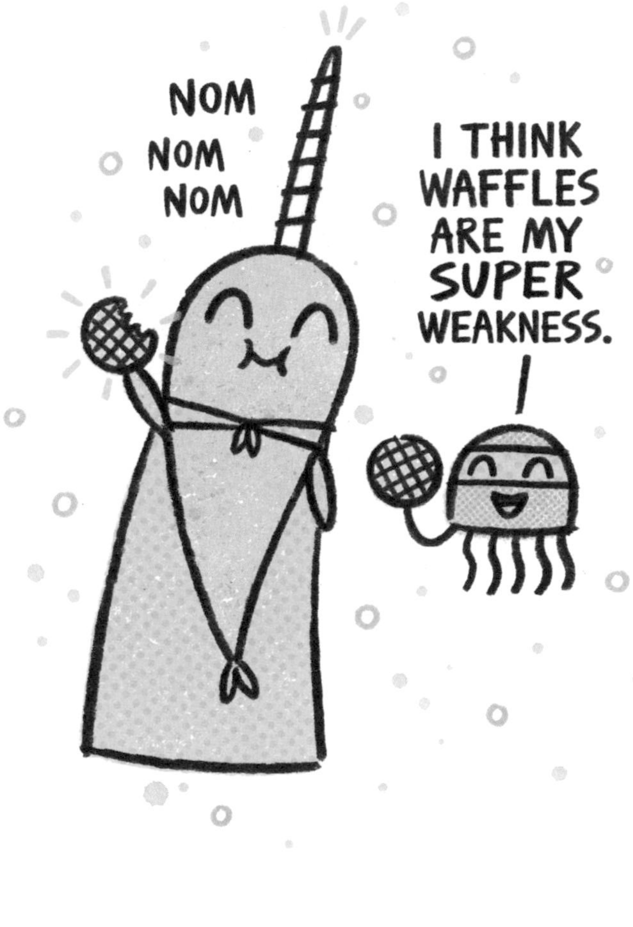
NOM
NOM
NOM
I THINK WAFFLES ARE MY SUPER WEAKNESS.

SUPER SEA CREATURES

REAL SEA CREATURES WITH REAL SUPER-AWESOME ABILITIES

THE MIMIC OCTOPUS CAN CHANGE ITS COLOR, SHAPE AND MOVEMENTS TO LOOK LIKE OTHER SEA LIFE SUCH AS SNAKES, LIONFISH, STINGRAYS AND JELLYFISH.

STOP COPYING ME!

STOP COPYING ME!

DOLPHINS SLEEP WITH ONLY HALF OF THEIR BRAIN AND WITH ONE EYE OPEN TO WATCH FOR THREATS.

DOLPHINS CAN ALSO "SEE" INSIDE MANY ANIMALS BY USING SOUND WAVES.

I SEE YOU HAD A WAFFLE FOR LUNCH!

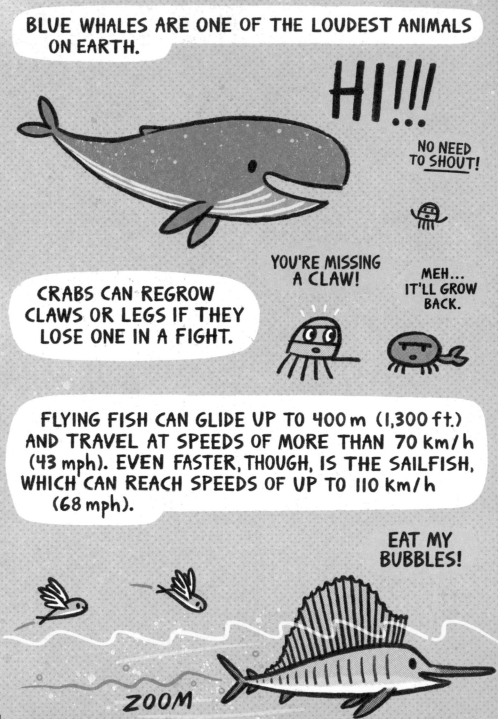

BLUE WHALES ARE ONE OF THE LOUDEST ANIMALS ON EARTH.

HI!!!...

NO NEED TO SHOUT!

CRABS CAN REGROW CLAWS OR LEGS IF THEY LOSE ONE IN A FIGHT.

YOU'RE MISSING A CLAW!

MEH... IT'LL GROW BACK.

FLYING FISH CAN GLIDE UP TO 400 m (1,300 ft.) AND TRAVEL AT SPEEDS OF MORE THAN 70 km/h (43 mph). EVEN FASTER, THOUGH, IS THE SAILFISH, WHICH CAN REACH SPEEDS OF UP TO 110 km/h (68 mph).

EAT MY BUBBLES!

ZOOM

NARWHAL, YOU'RE

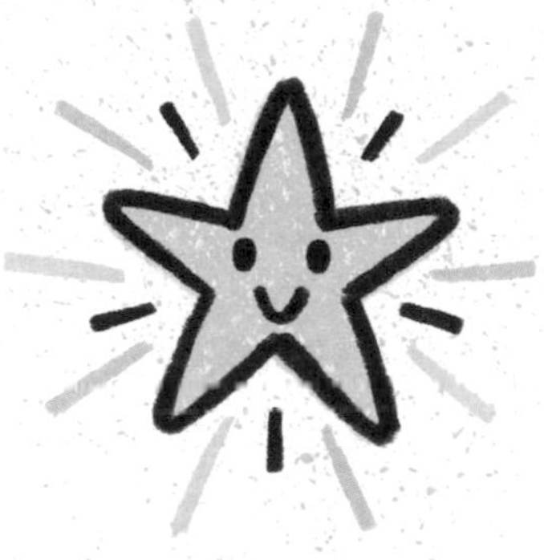

A SUPERSTAR!

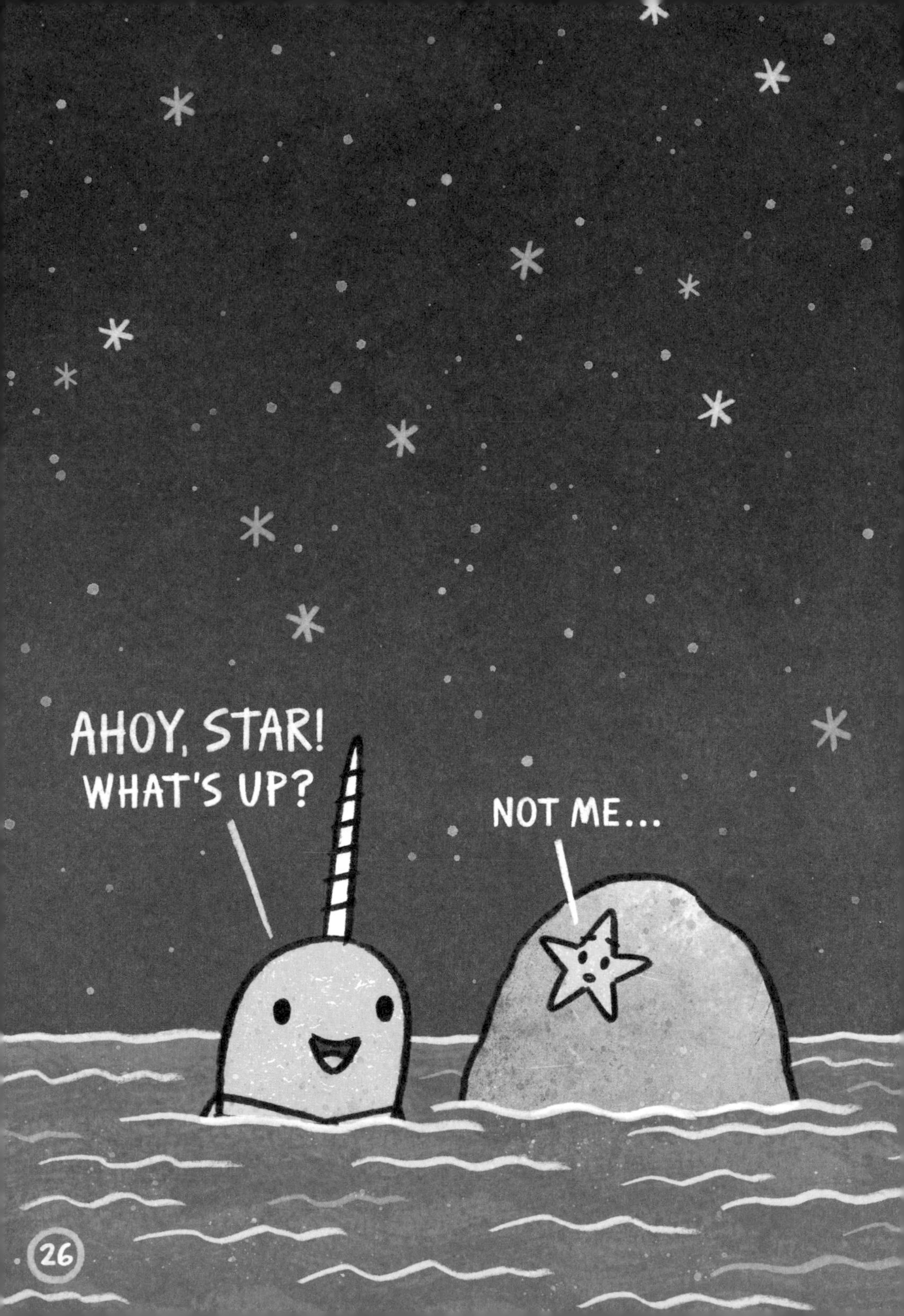
AHOY, STAR! WHAT'S UP?
NOT ME...

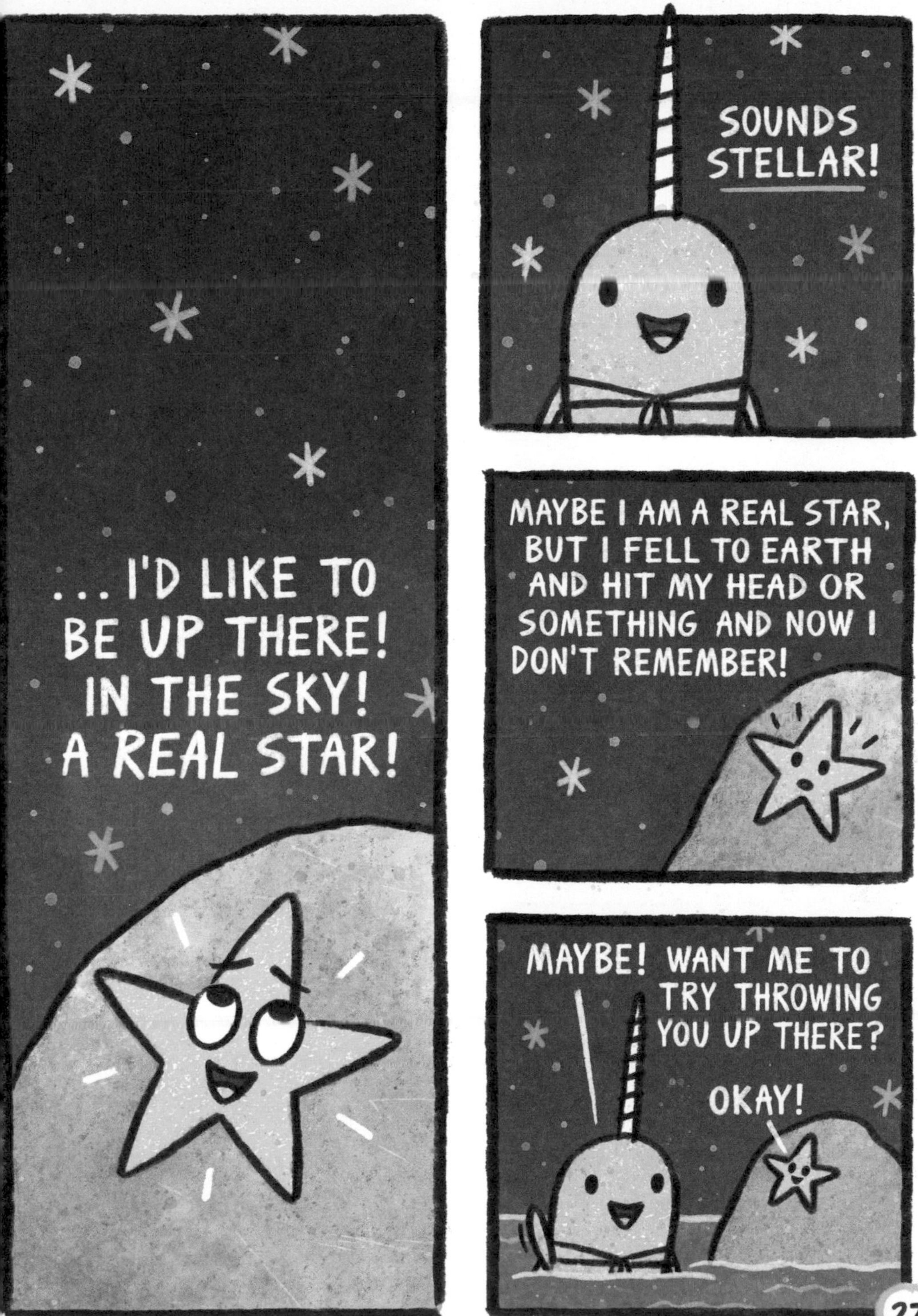
...I'D LIKE TO BE UP THERE! IN THE SKY! A REAL STAR!
SOUNDS STELLAR!
MAYBE I AM A REAL STAR, BUT I FELL TO EARTH AND HIT MY HEAD OR SOMETHING AND NOW I DON'T REMEMBER!
MAYBE! WANT ME TO TRY THROWING YOU UP THERE?
OKAY!

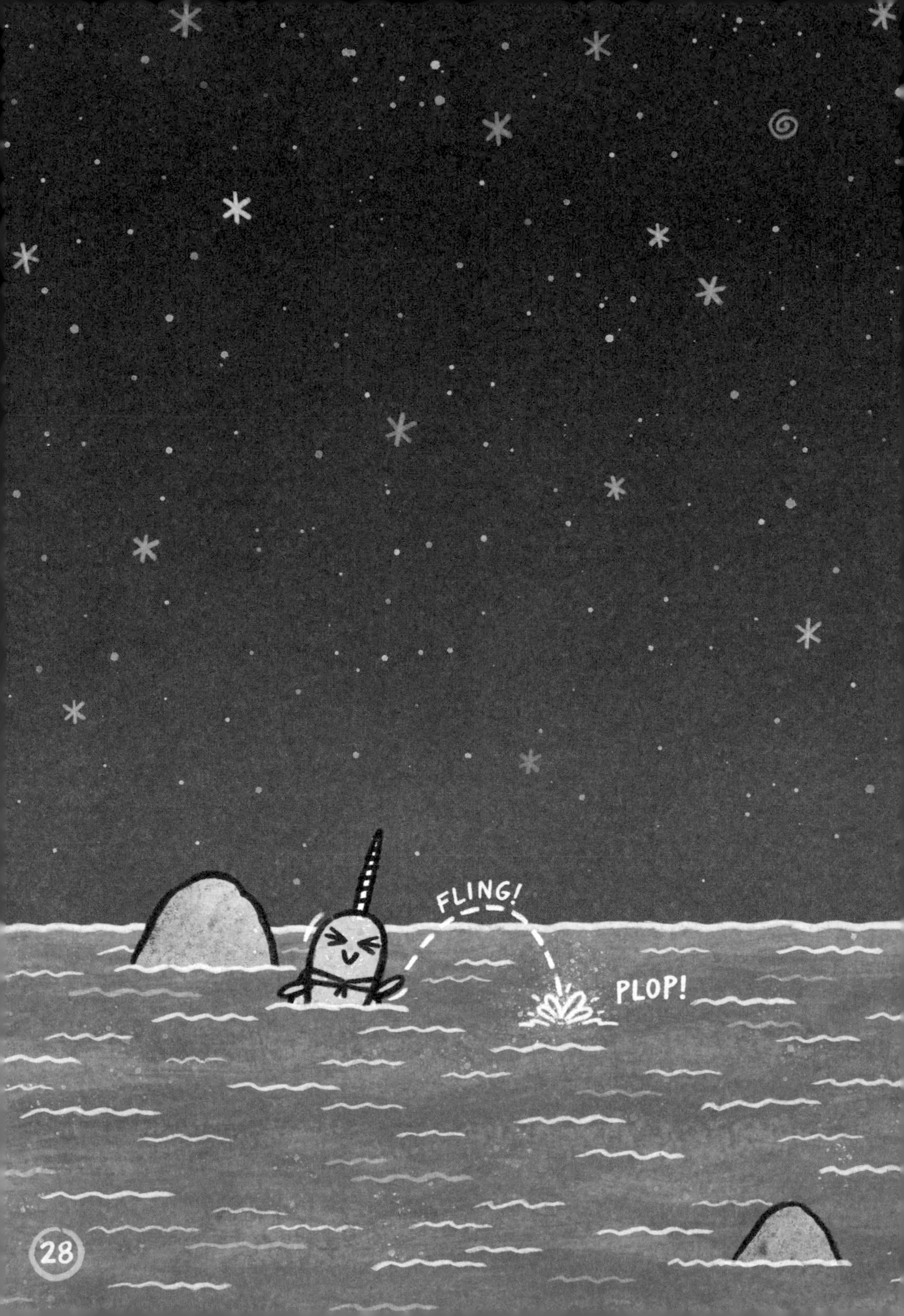
FLING!
PLOP!

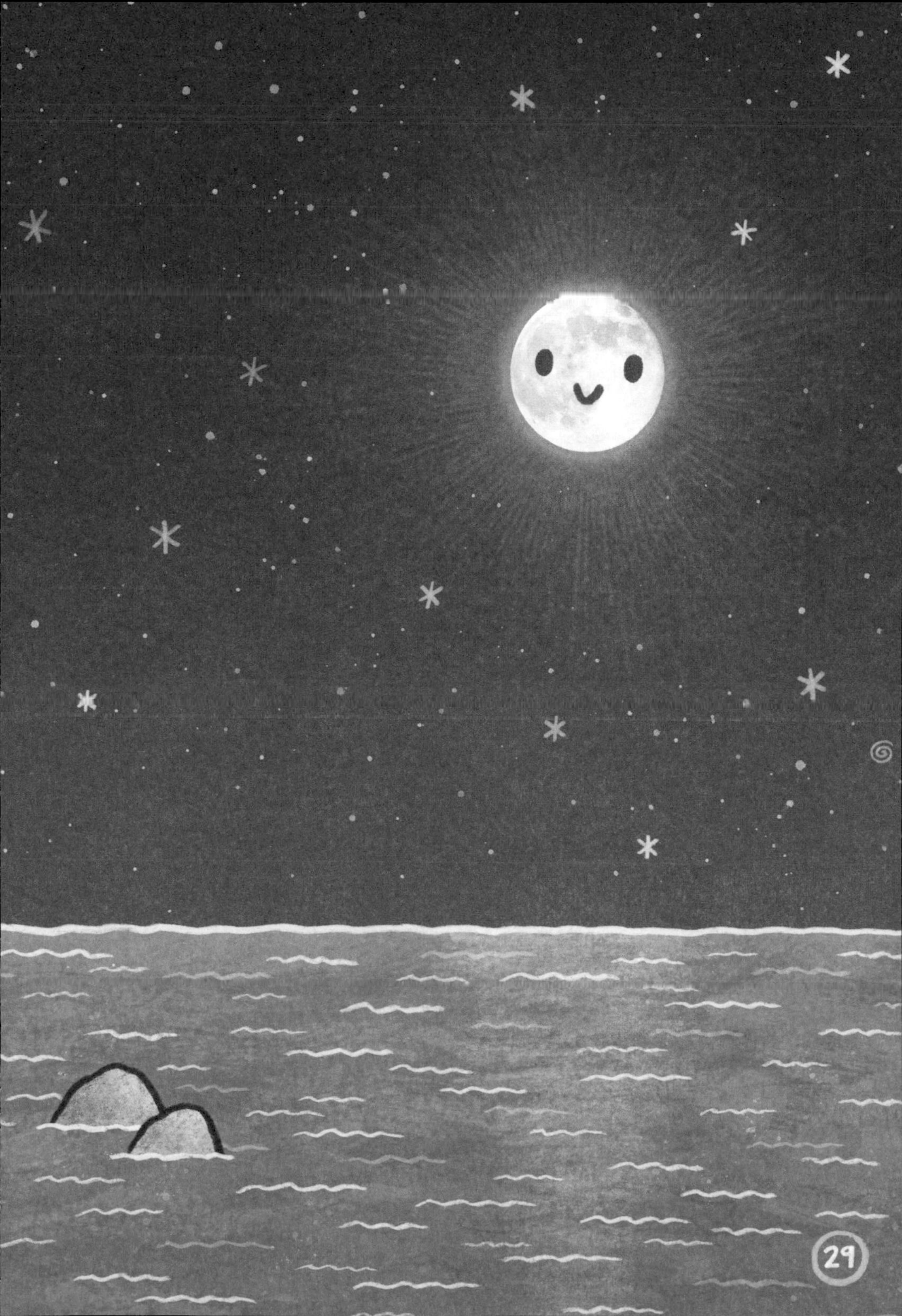

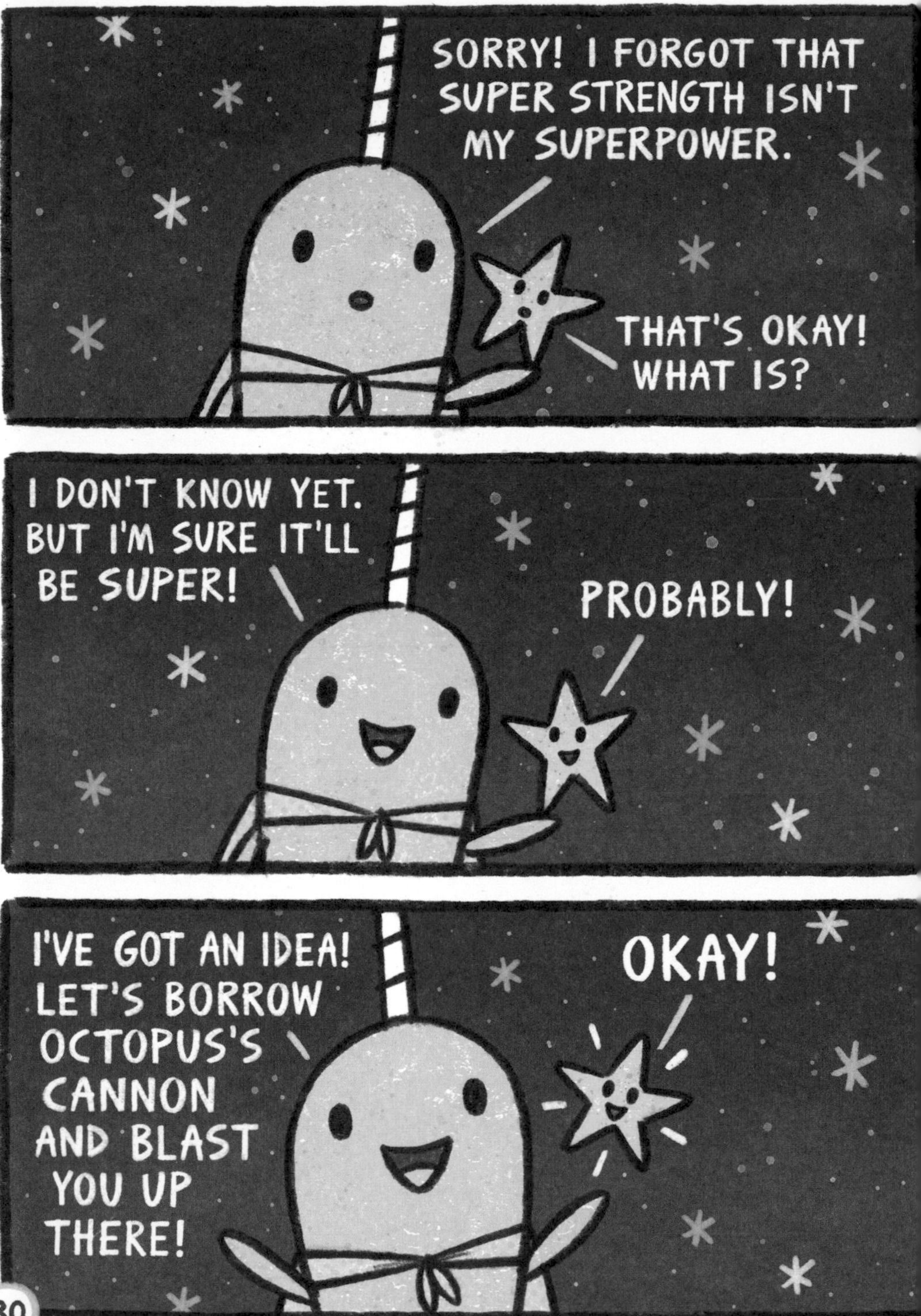
SORRY! I FORGOT THAT SUPER STRENGTH ISN'T MY SUPERPOWER.
THAT'S OKAY! WHAT IS?
I DON'T KNOW YET. BUT I'M SURE IT'LL BE SUPER!
PROBABLY!
I'VE GOT AN IDEA! LET'S BORROW OCTOPUS'S CANNON AND BLAST YOU UP THERE!
OKAY!

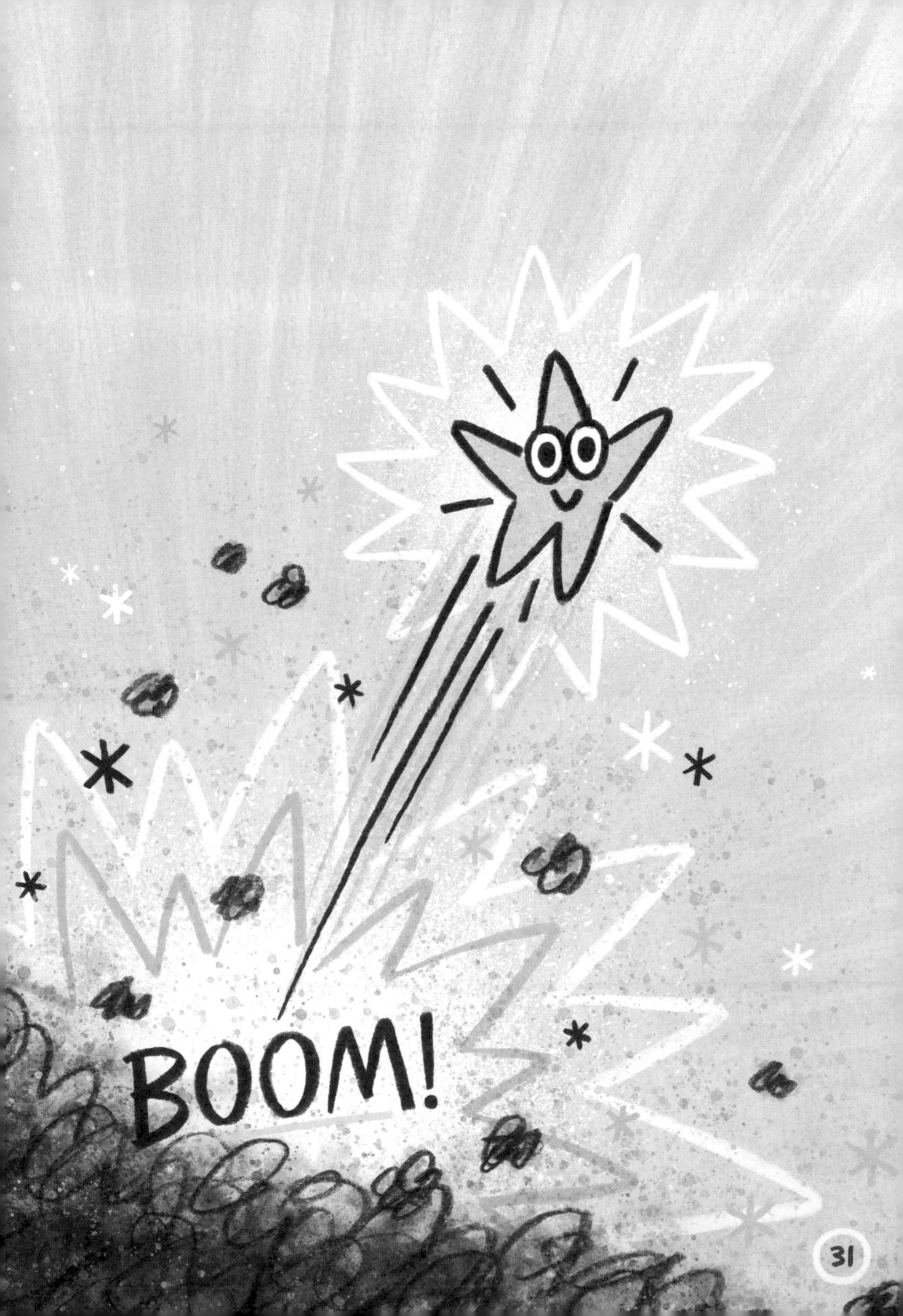
BOOM!

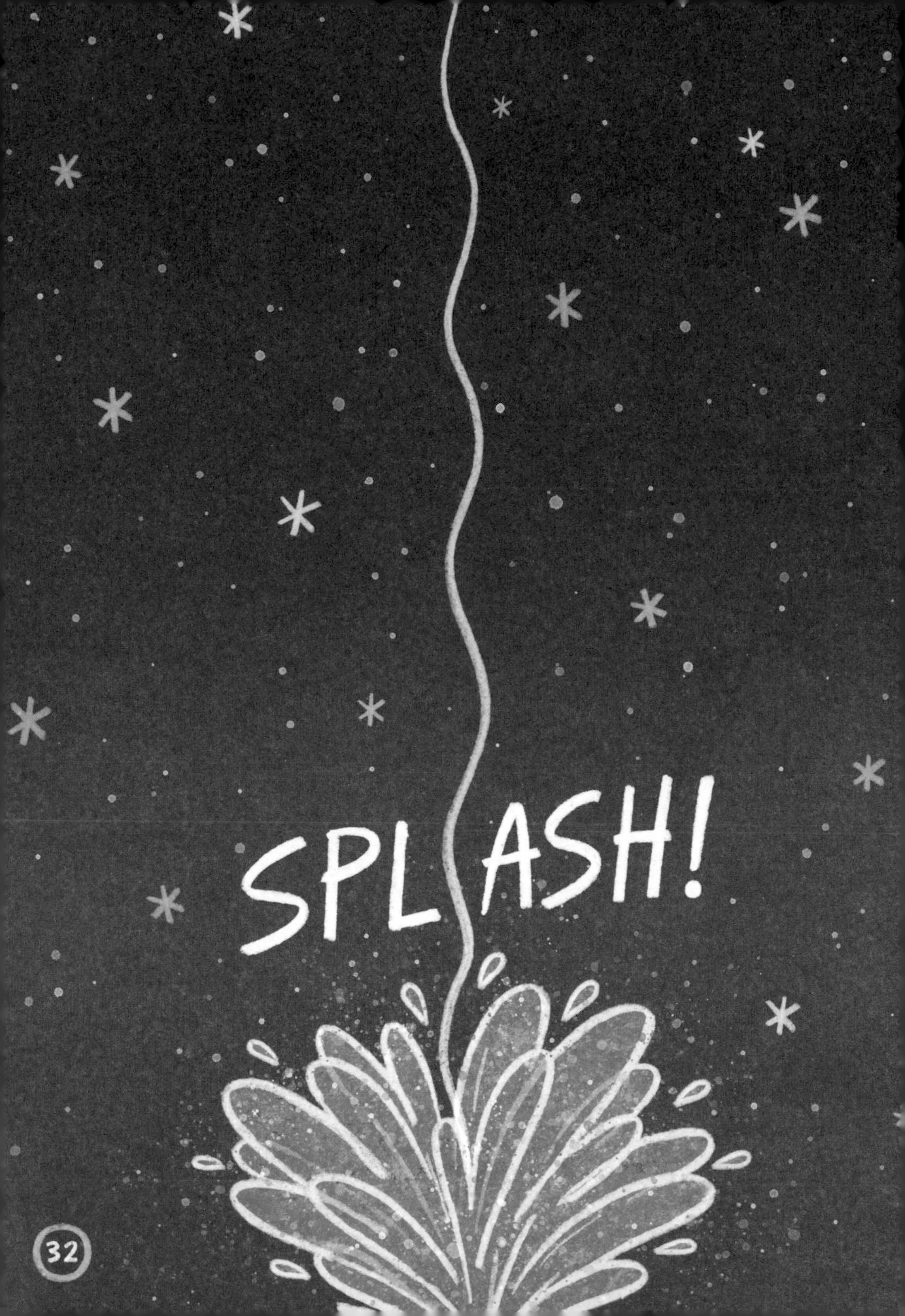
SPLASH!

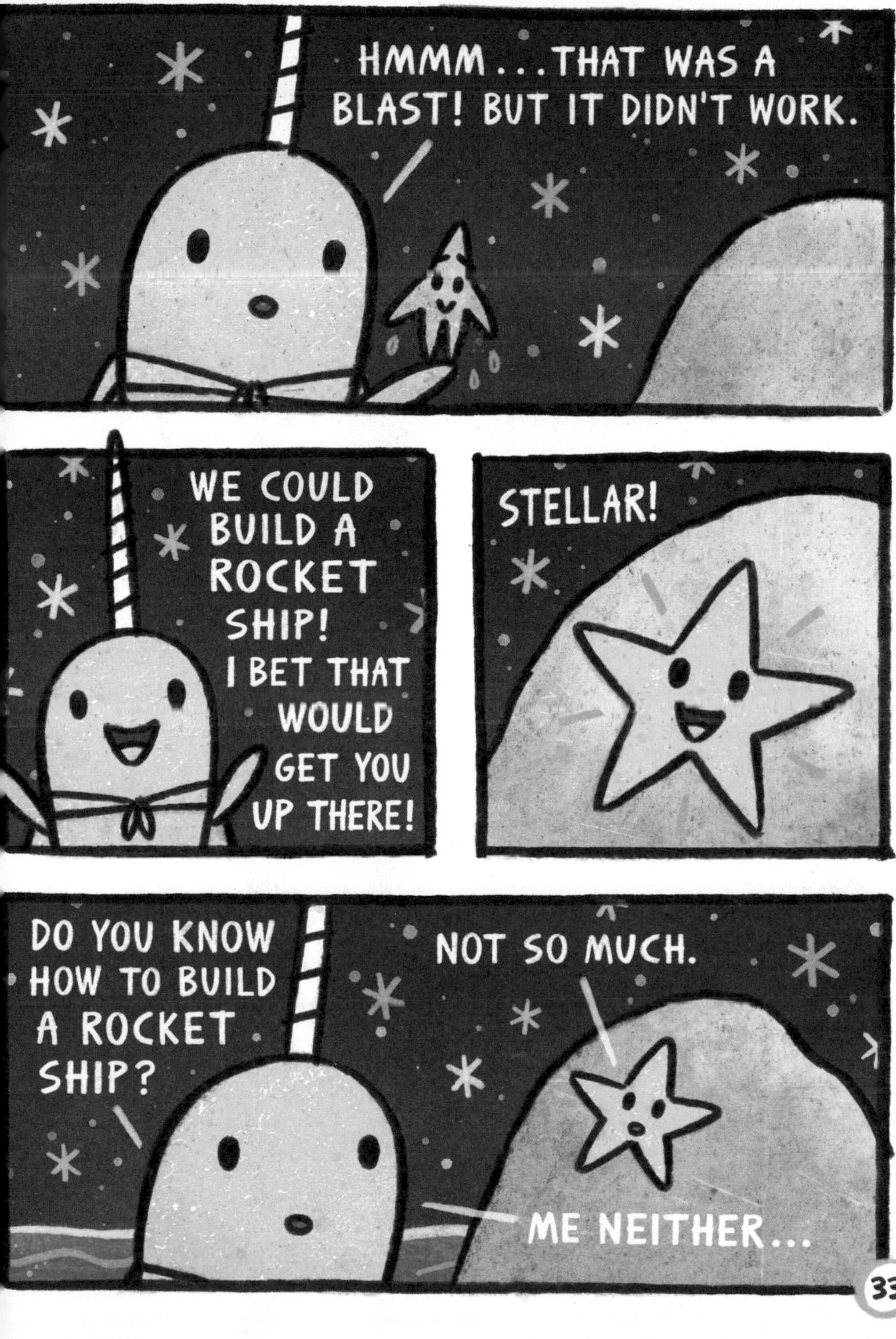
HMMM...THAT WAS A BLAST! BUT IT DIDN'T WORK.
WE COULD BUILD A ROCKET SHIP! I BET THAT WOULD GET YOU UP THERE!
STELLAR!
DO YOU KNOW HOW TO BUILD A ROCKET SHIP?
NOT SO MUCH.
ME NEITHER...

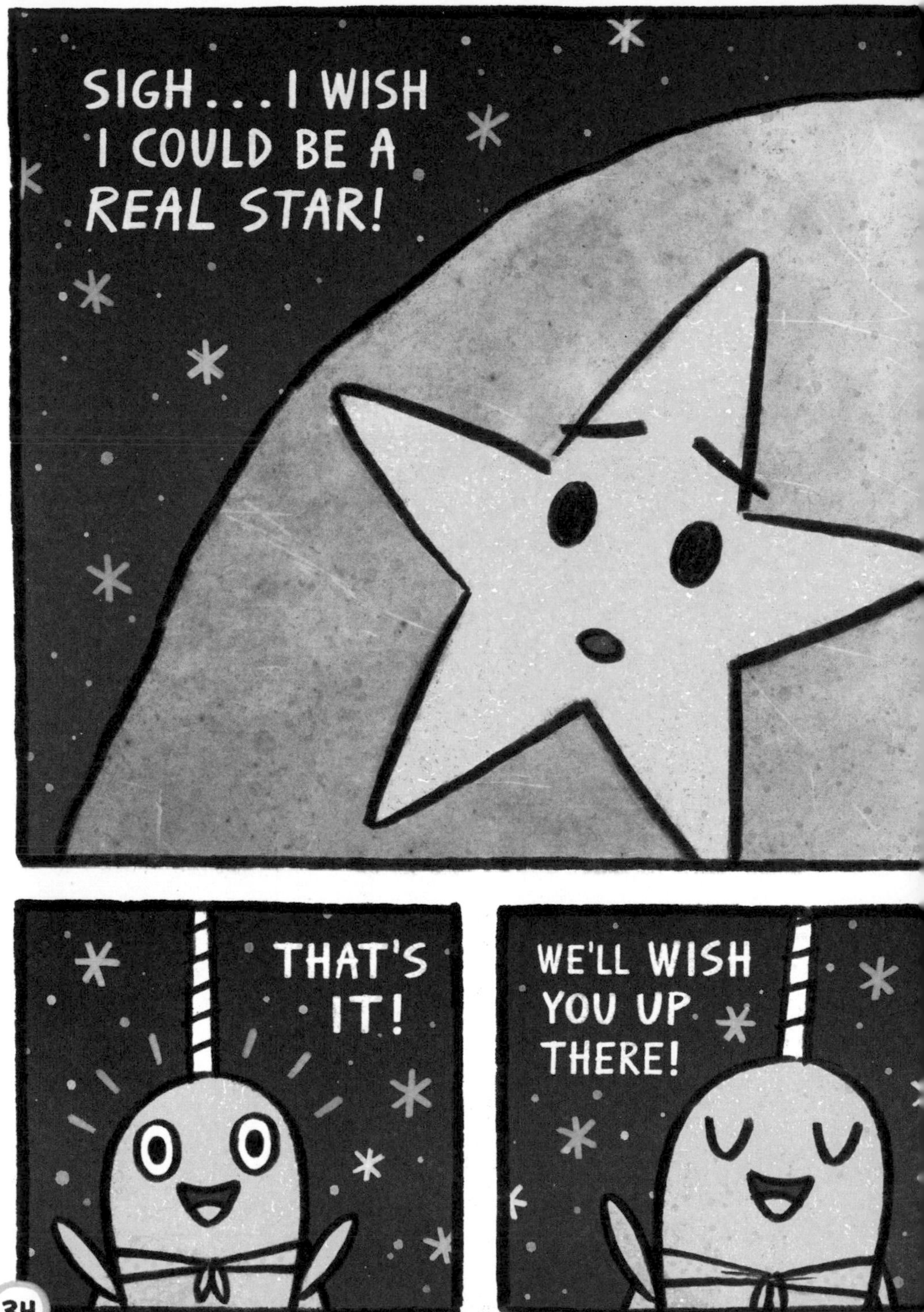
SIGH...I WISH I COULD BE A *REAL* STAR!
THAT'S IT!
WE'LL WISH YOU UP THERE!

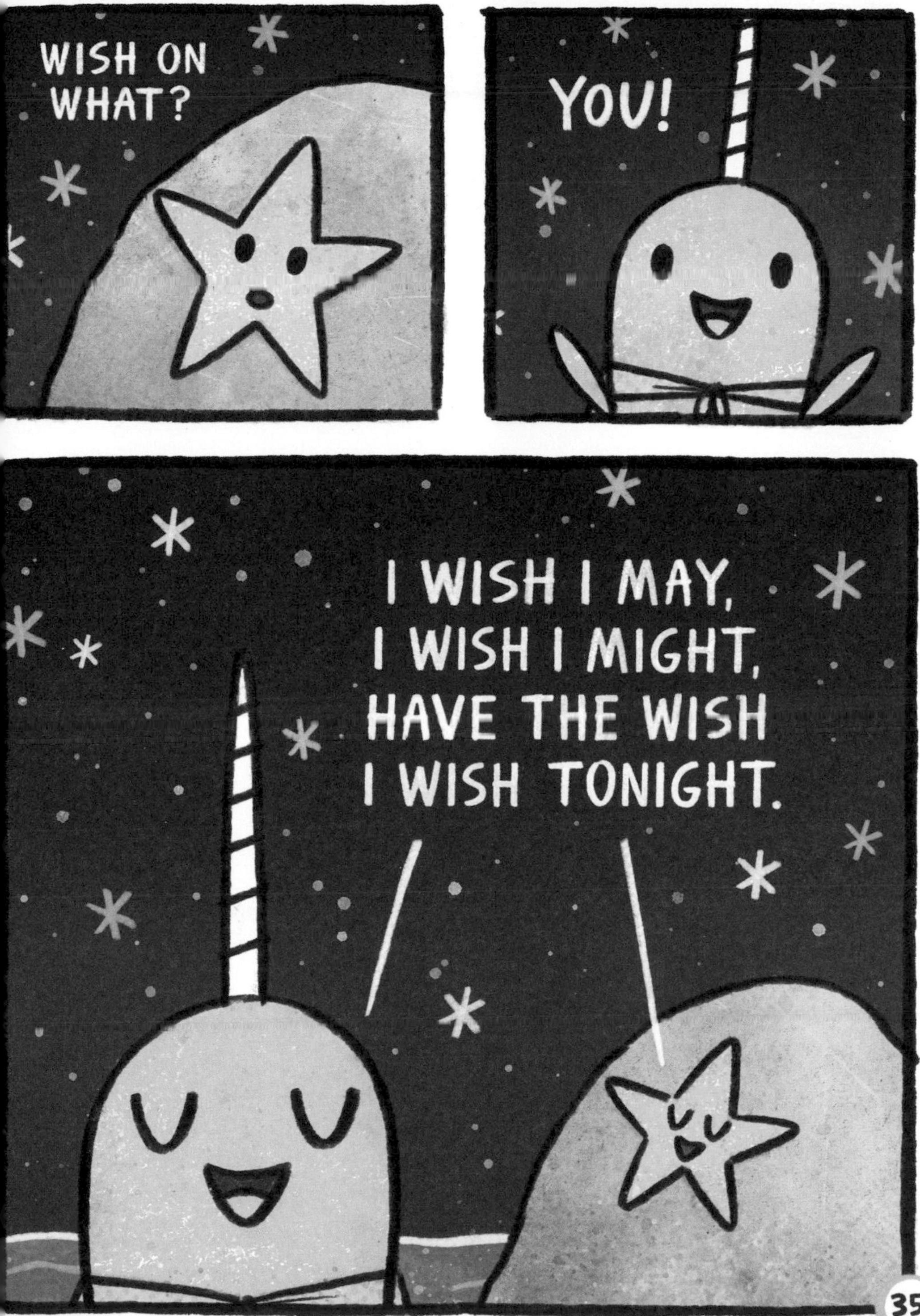

WISH ON WHAT?
YOU!
I WISH I MAY, I WISH I MIGHT, HAVE THE WISH I WISH TONIGHT.

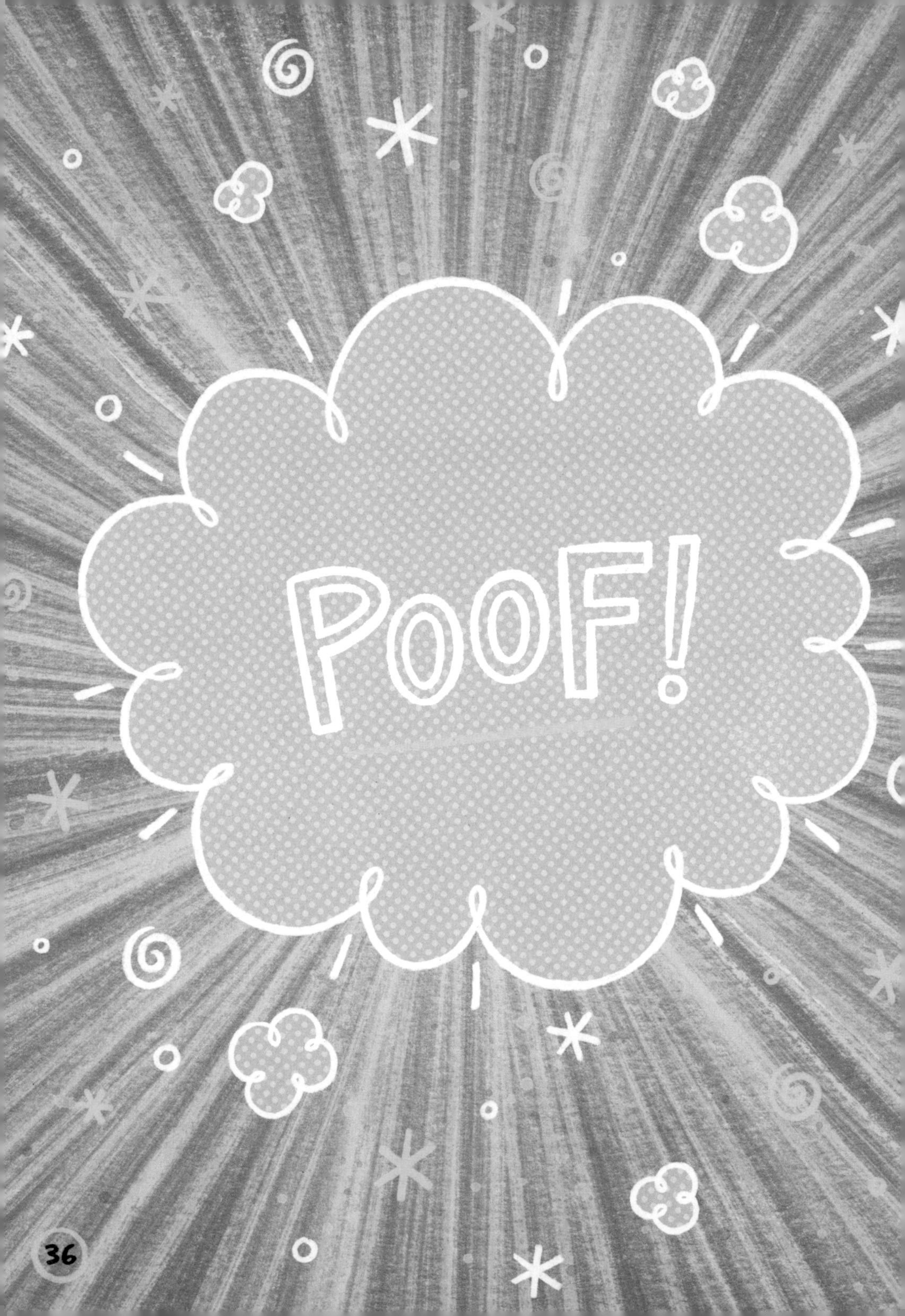
POOF!

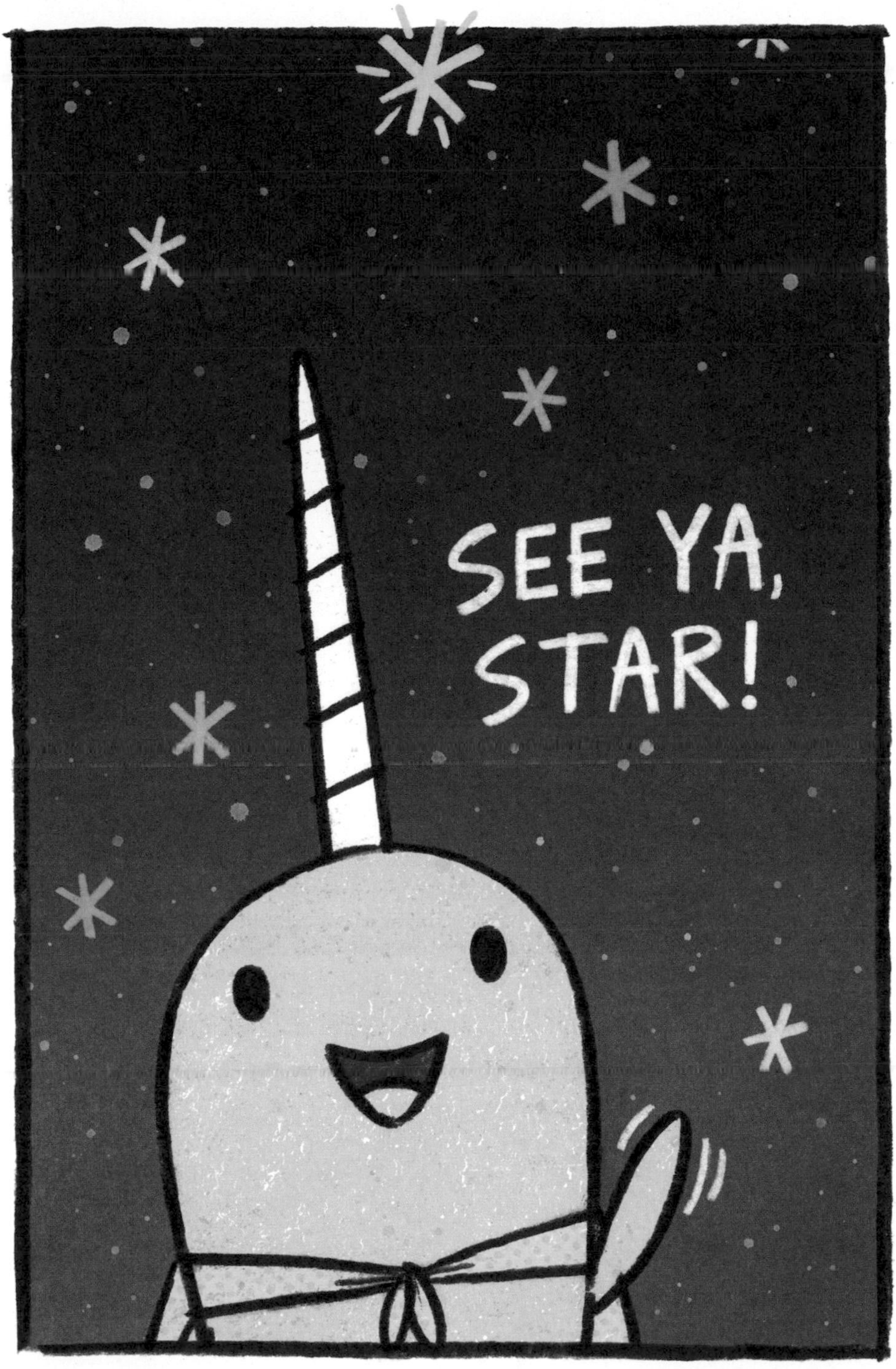
SEE YA, STAR!

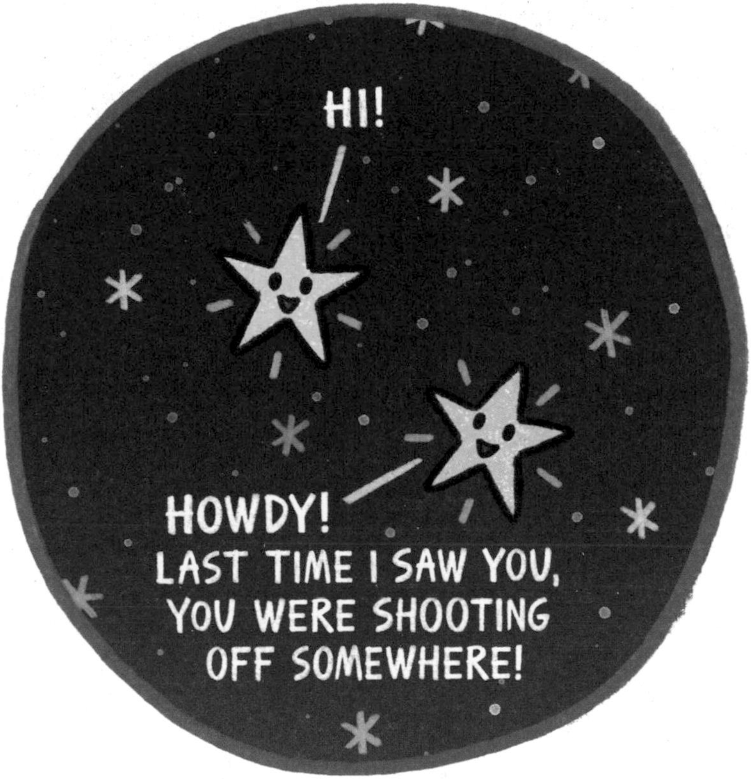
HI!
HOWDY!
LAST TIME I SAW YOU, YOU WERE SHOOTING OFF SOMEWHERE!

SUPER WAFFLE AND STRAWBERRY SIDEKICK!

by Narwhal and Jelly

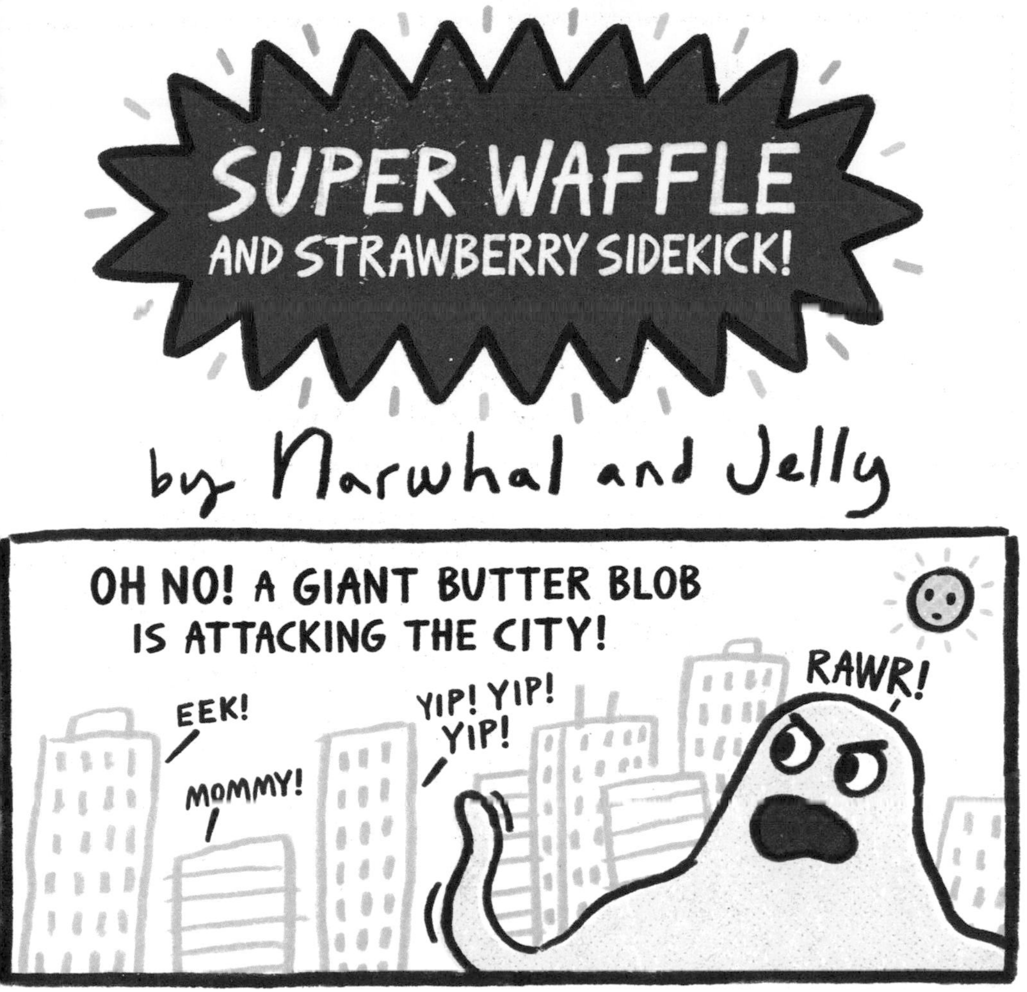
OH NO! A GIANT BUTTER BLOB IS ATTACKING THE CITY!
EEK!
MOMMY!
YIP! YIP! YIP!
RAWR!

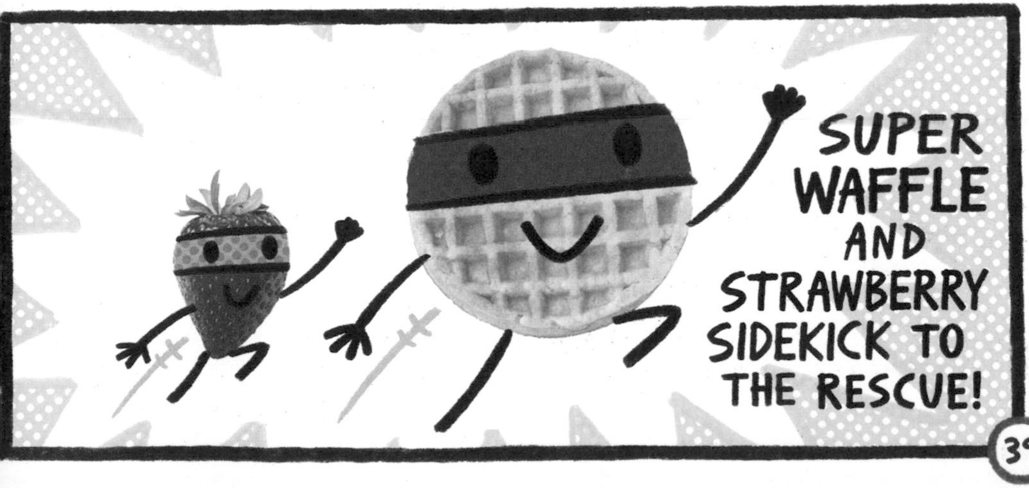
SUPER WAFFLE AND STRAWBERRY SIDEKICK TO THE RESCUE!

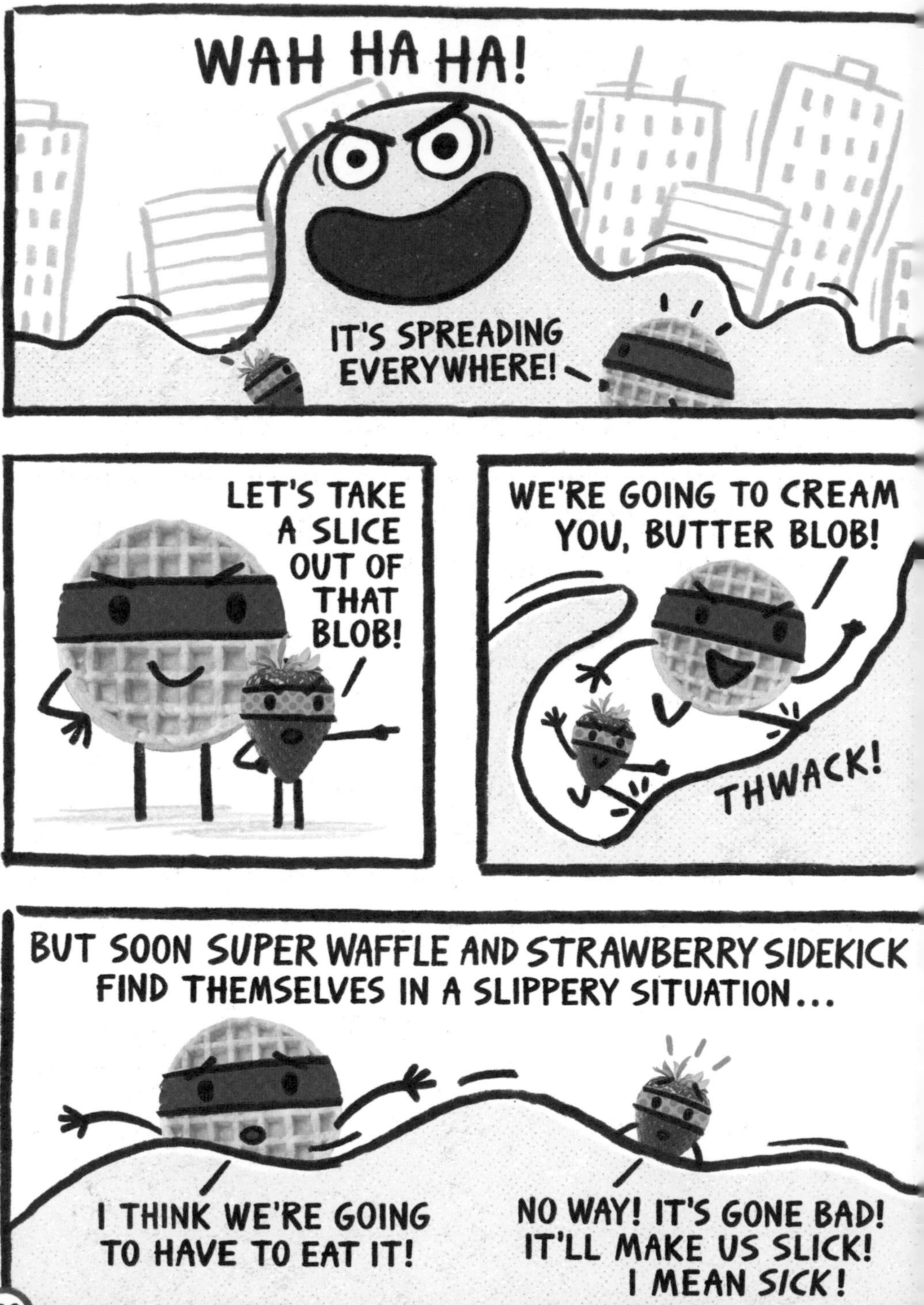
WAH HA HA!
IT'S SPREADING EVERYWHERE!
LET'S TAKE A SLICE OUT OF THAT BLOB!
WE'RE GOING TO CREAM YOU, BUTTER BLOB!
THWACK!
BUT SOON SUPER WAFFLE AND STRAWBERRY SIDEKICK FIND THEMSELVES IN A SLIPPERY SITUATION...
I THINK WE'RE GOING TO HAVE TO EAT IT!
NO WAY! IT'S GONE BAD! IT'LL MAKE US SLICK! I MEAN *SICK*!

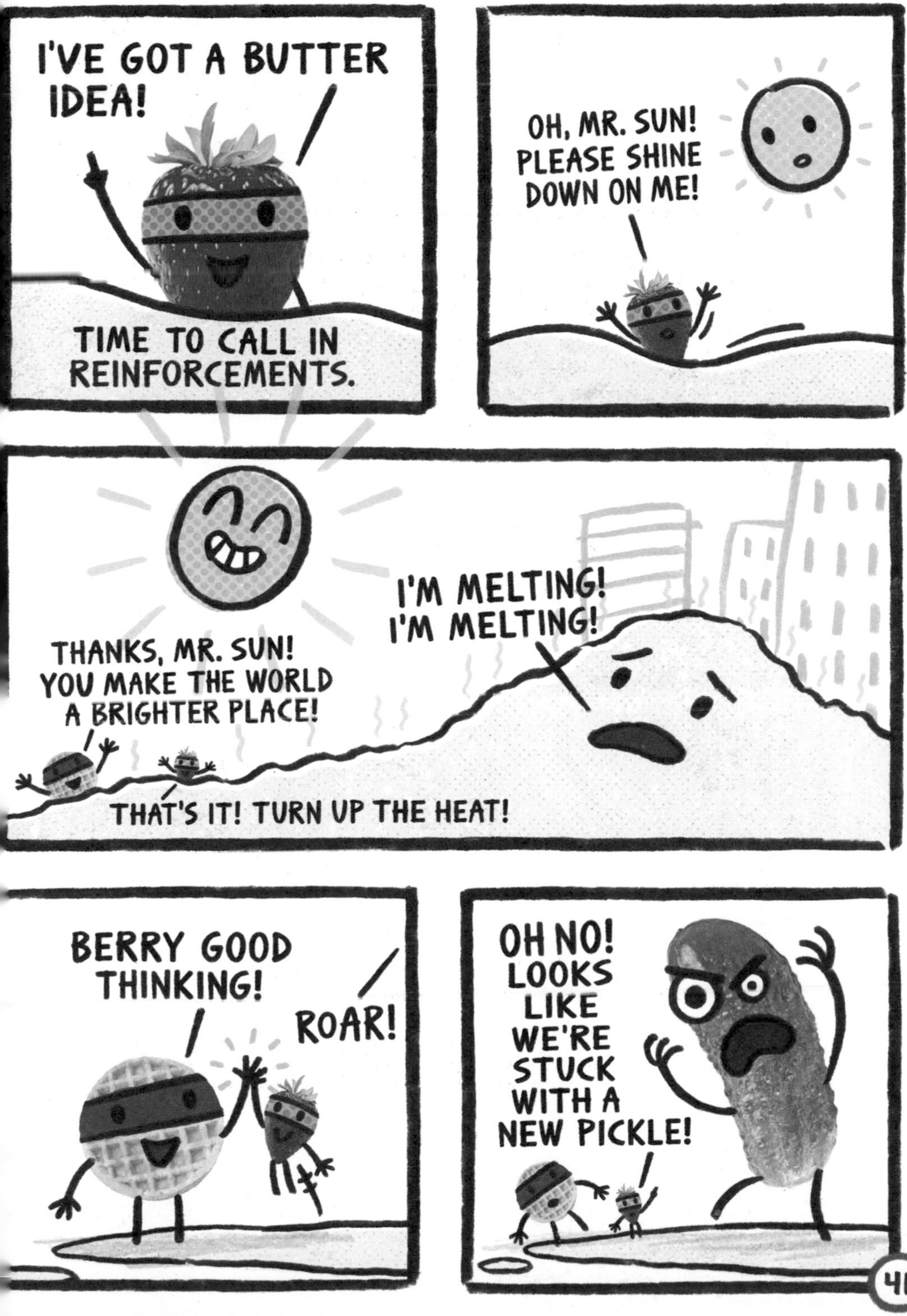
I'VE GOT A BUTTER IDEA!
TIME TO CALL IN REINFORCEMENTS.
OH, MR. SUN! PLEASE SHINE DOWN ON ME!
THANKS, MR. SUN! YOU MAKE THE WORLD A BRIGHTER PLACE!
THAT'S IT! TURN UP THE HEAT!
I'M MELTING! I'M MELTING!
BERRY GOOD THINKING!
ROAR!
OH NO! LOOKS LIKE WE'RE STUCK WITH A NEW PICKLE!

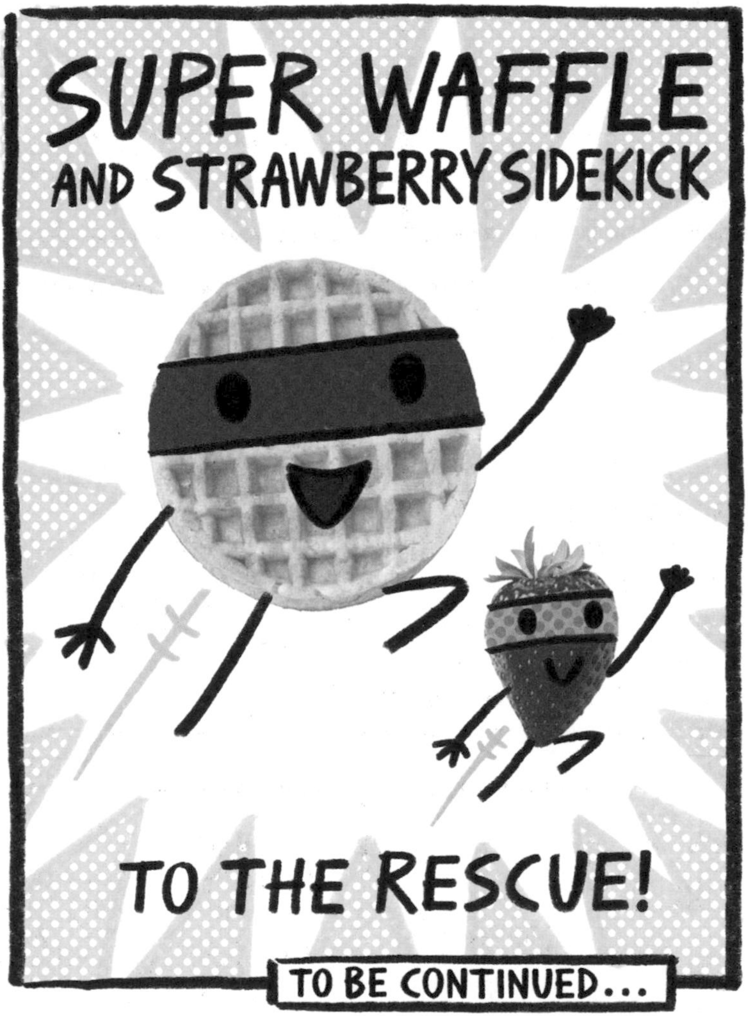
SUPER WAFFLE
AND STRAWBERRY SIDEKICK
TO THE RESCUE!
TO BE CONTINUED...

SUPER NARWHAL VS. BLUE JELLY

A.K.A.

THE SUPER SUPERPOWER!

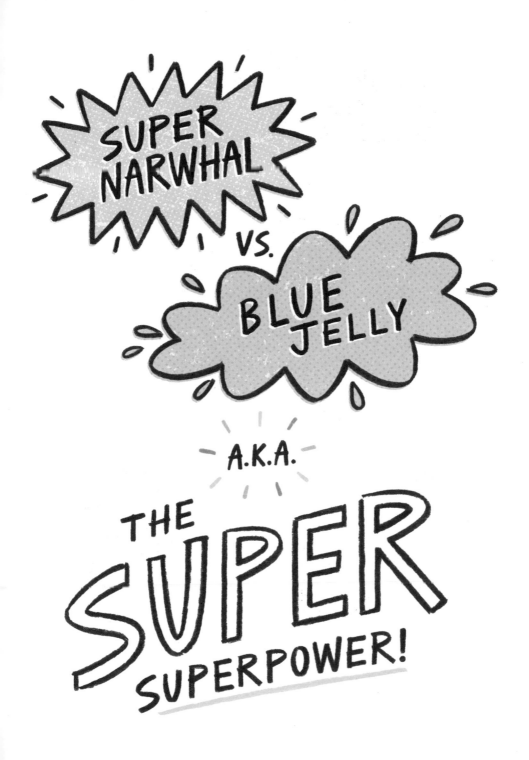

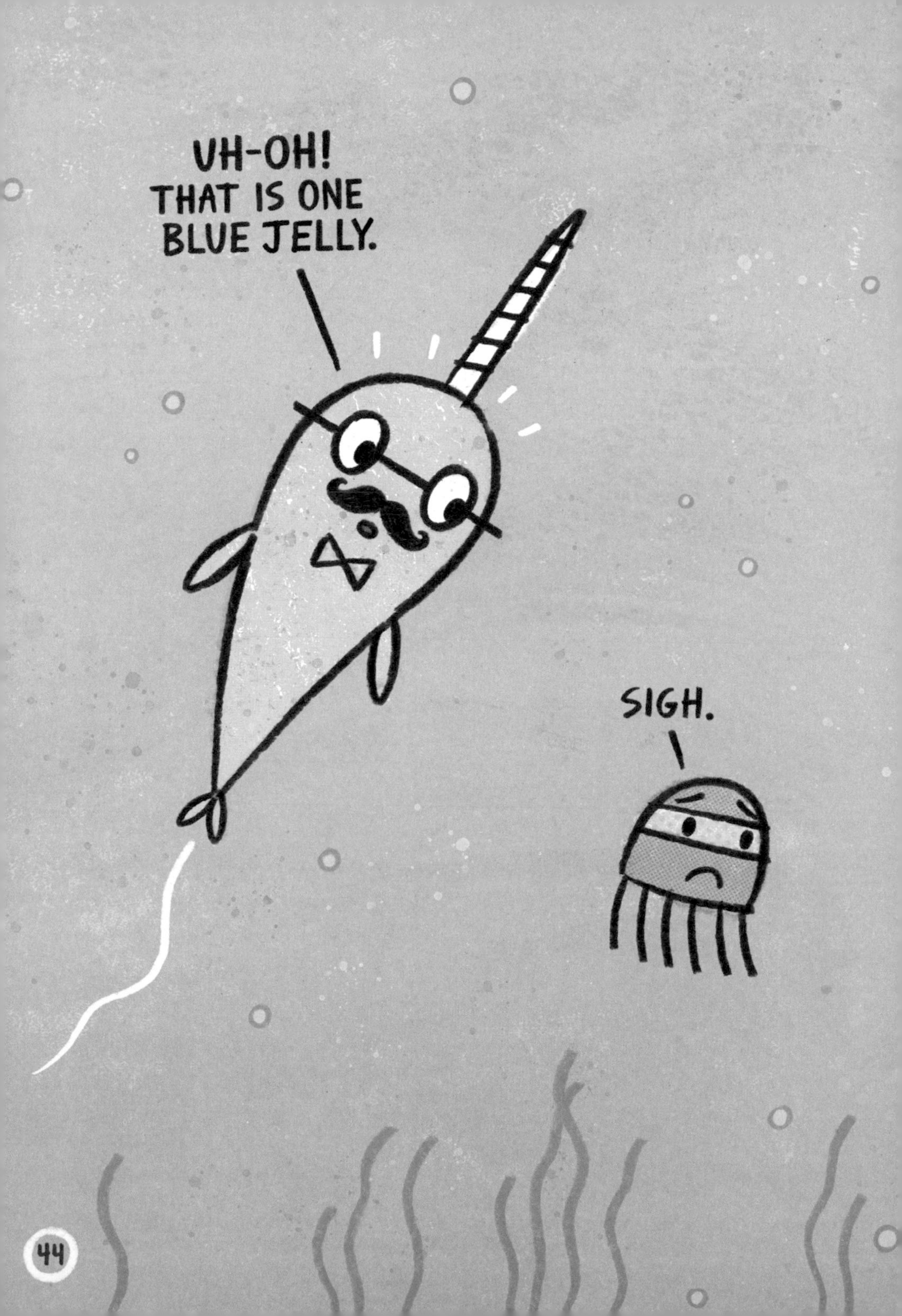
UH-OH!
THAT IS ONE
BLUE JELLY.
SIGH.

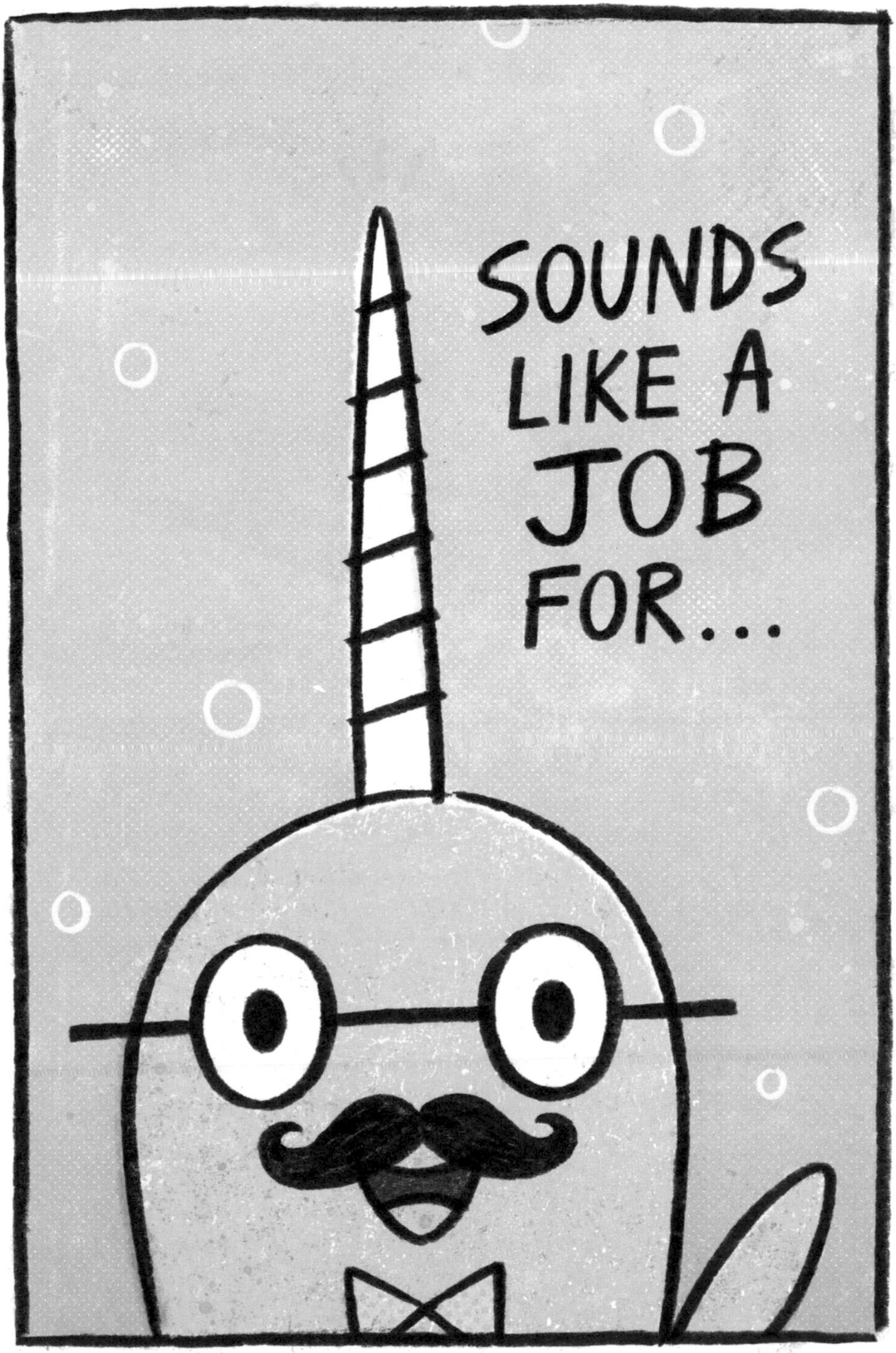
SOUNDS LIKE A JOB FOR...

SUPER NARWHAL!

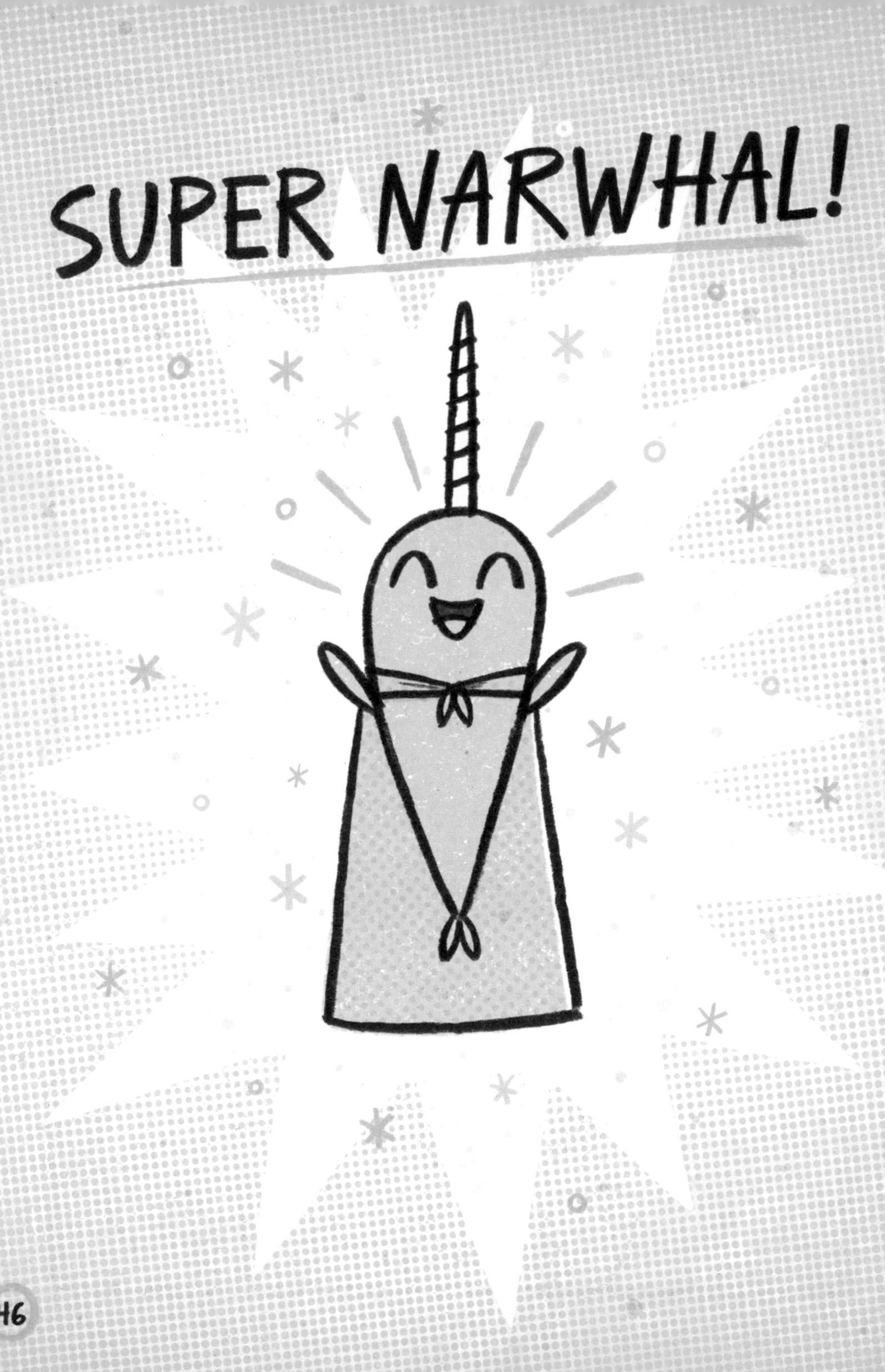

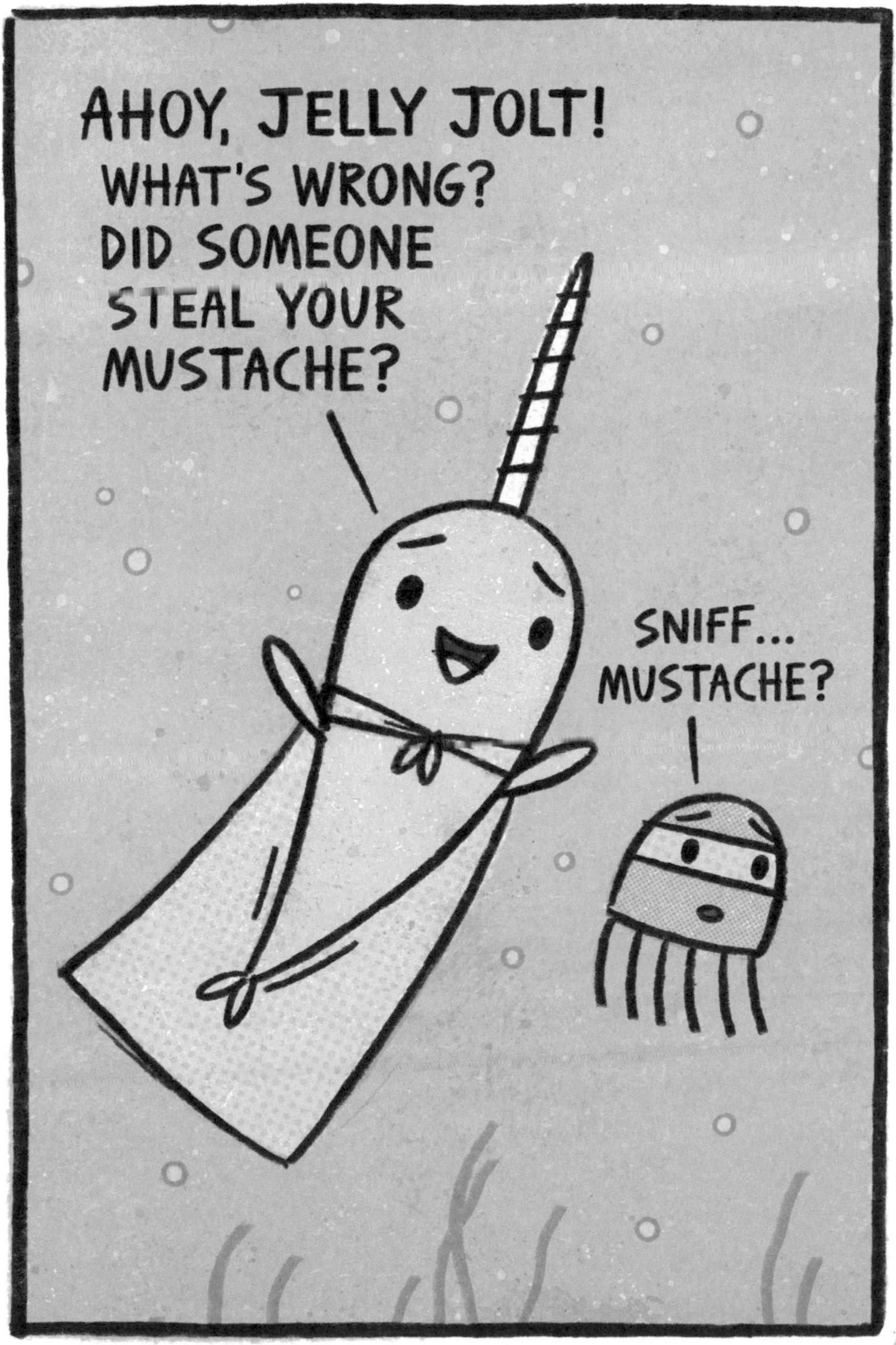
AHOY, JELLY JOLT!
WHAT'S WRONG? DID SOMEONE STEAL YOUR MUSTACHE?
SNIFF... MUSTACHE?

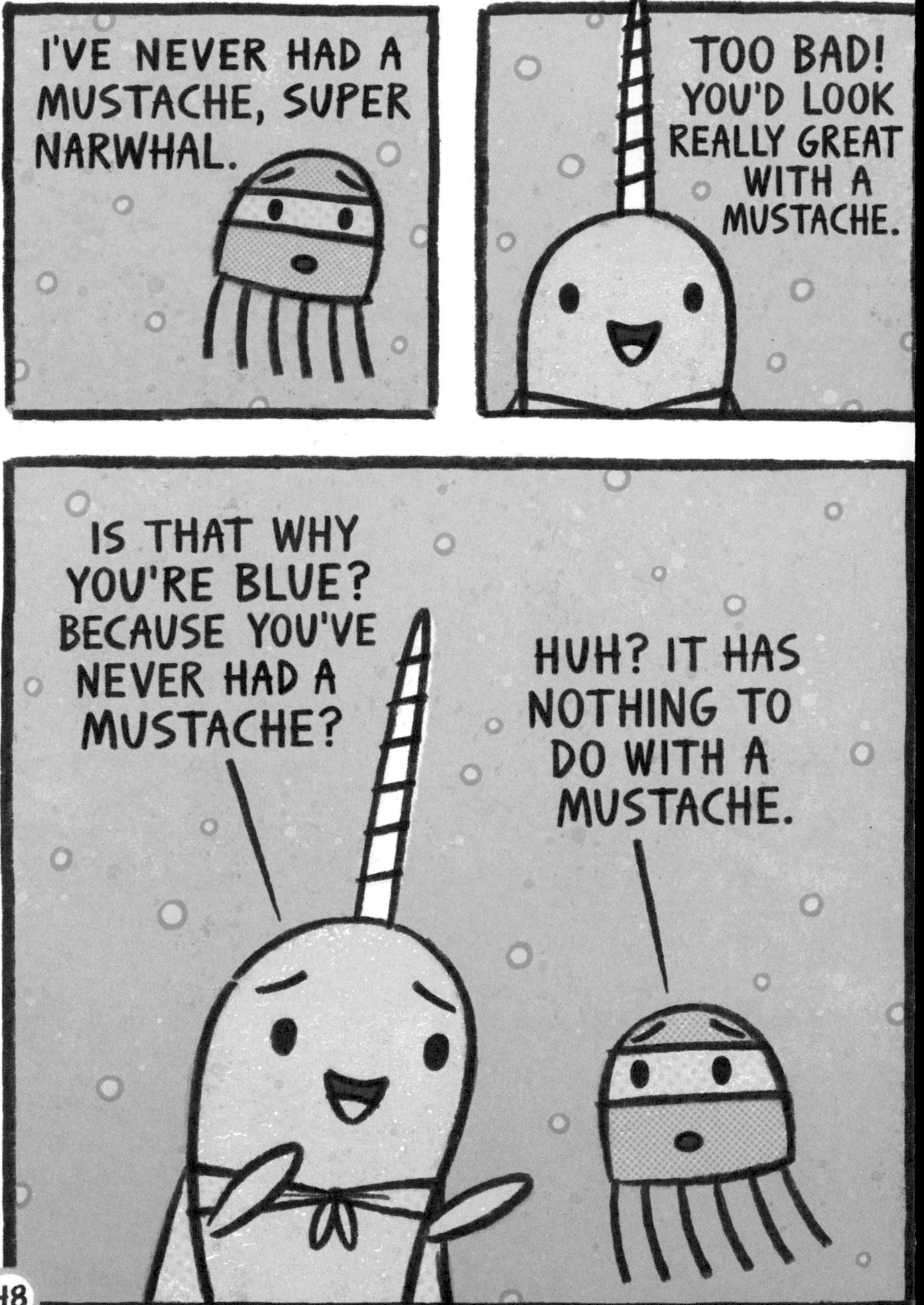
I'VE NEVER HAD A MUSTACHE, SUPER NARWHAL.
TOO BAD! YOU'D LOOK REALLY GREAT WITH A MUSTACHE.
IS THAT WHY YOU'RE BLUE? BECAUSE YOU'VE NEVER HAD A MUSTACHE?
HUH? IT HAS NOTHING TO DO WITH A MUSTACHE.

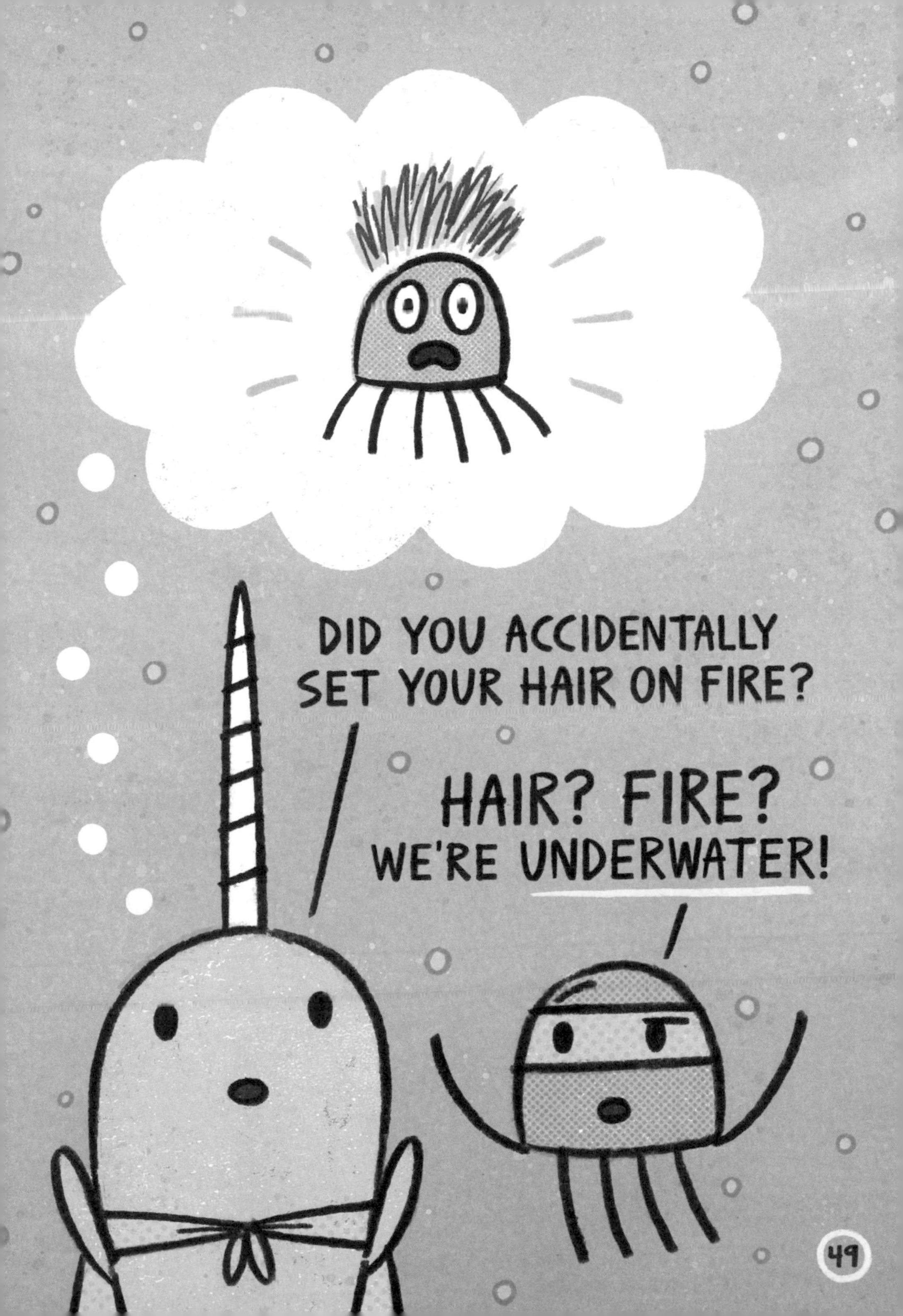
DID YOU ACCIDENTALLY SET YOUR HAIR ON FIRE?
HAIR? FIRE? WE'RE UNDERWATER!

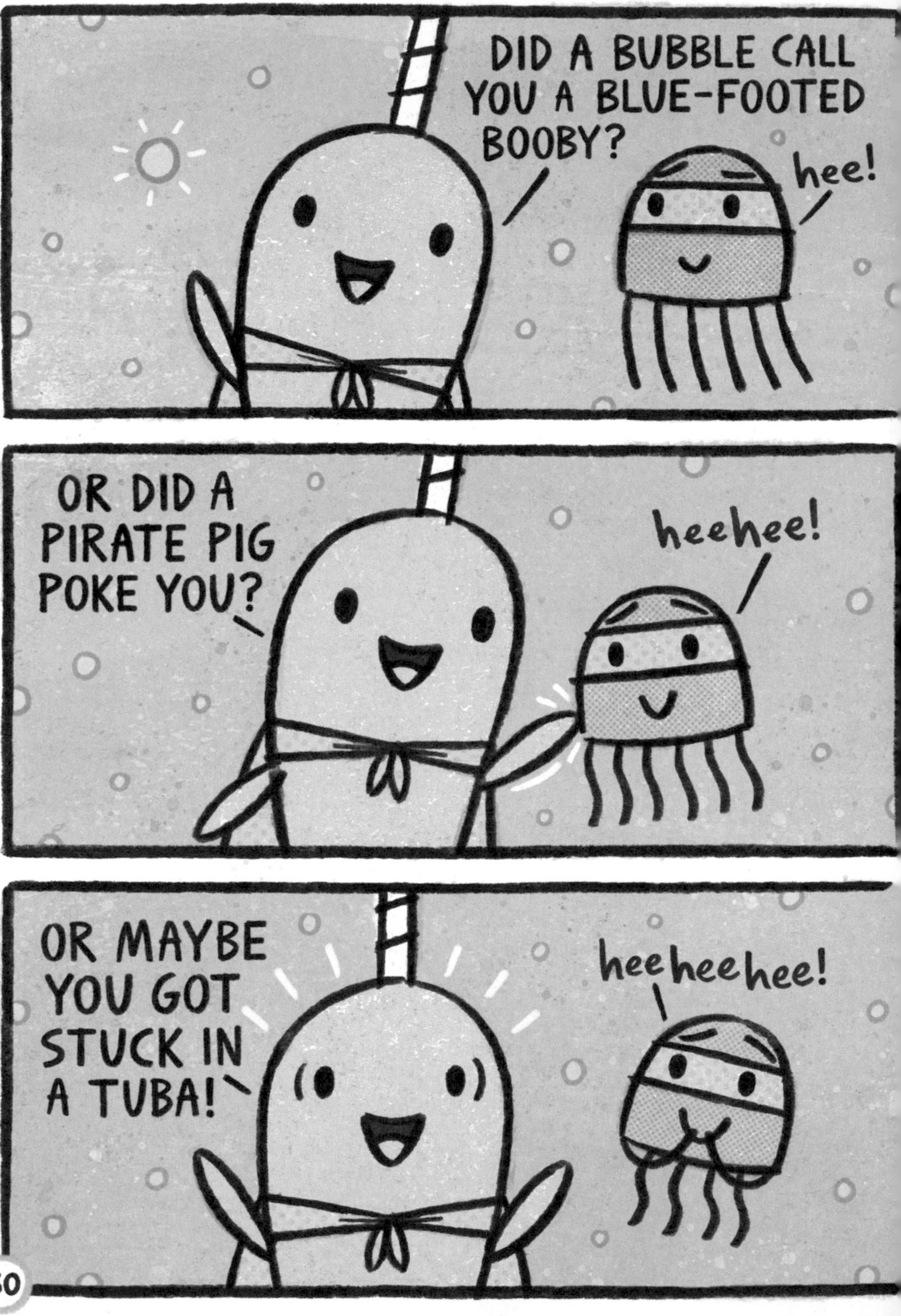
DID A BUBBLE CALL YOU A BLUE-FOOTED BOOBY?
hee!
OR DID A PIRATE PIG POKE YOU?
heehee!
OR MAYBE YOU GOT STUCK IN A TUBA!
heeheehee!

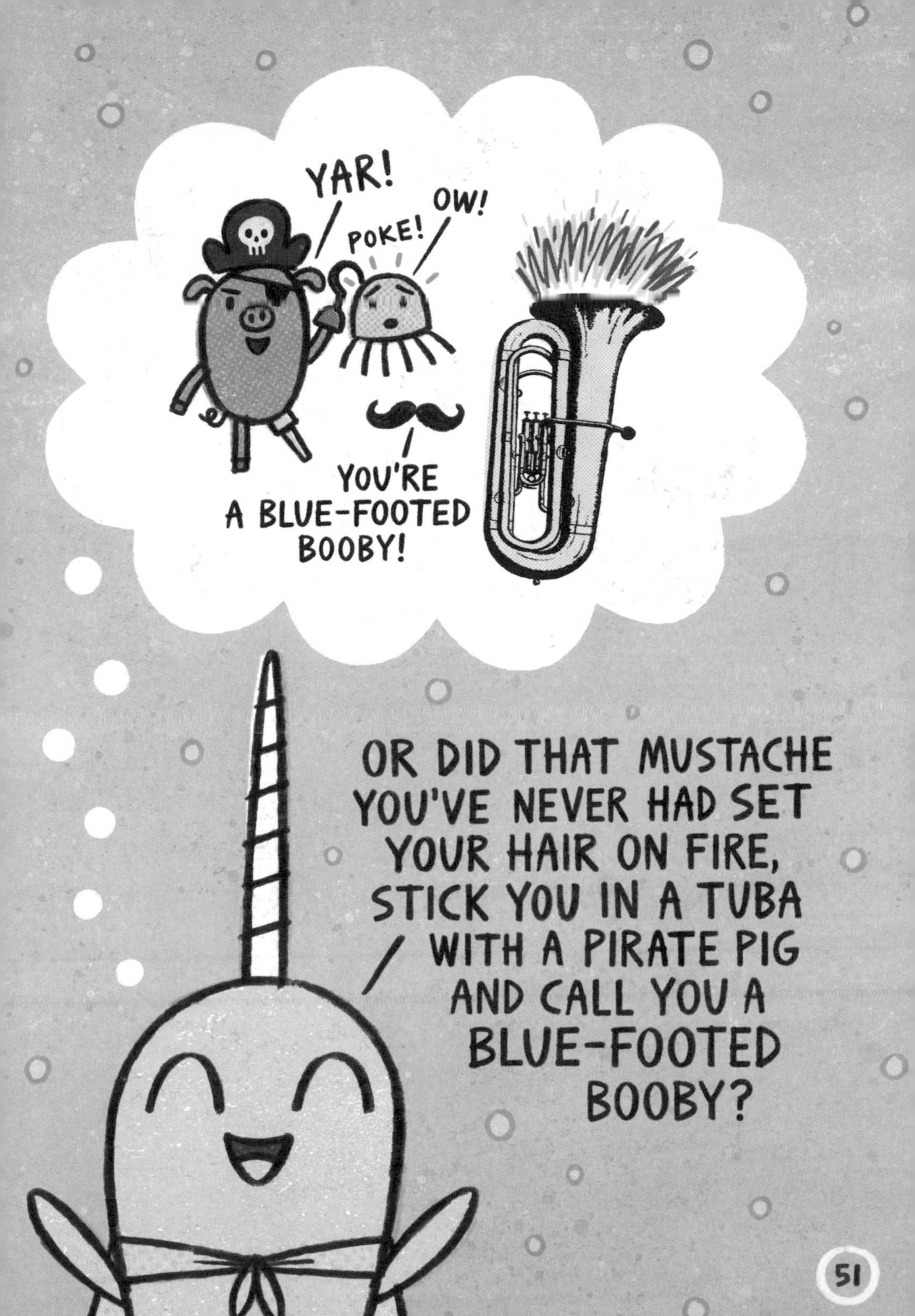
YAR!
POKE!
OW!
YOU'RE A BLUE-FOOTED BOOBY!
OR DID THAT MUSTACHE YOU'VE NEVER HAD SET YOUR HAIR ON FIRE, STICK YOU IN A TUBA WITH A PIRATE PIG AND CALL YOU A BLUE-FOOTED BOOBY?

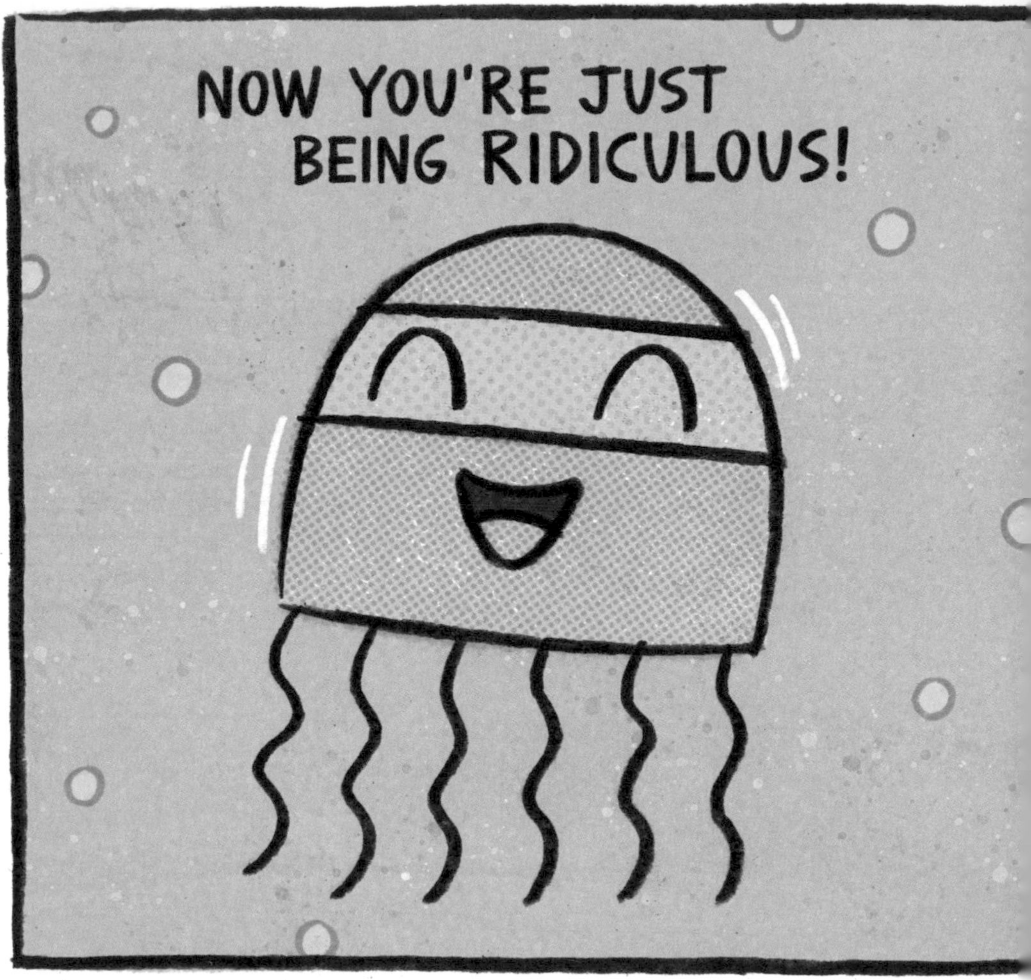
NOW YOU'RE JUST BEING RIDICULOUS!

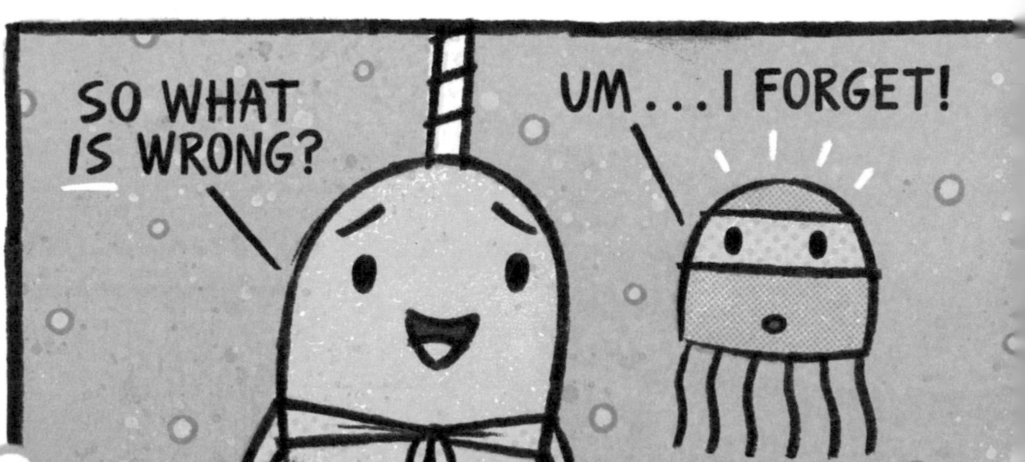
SO WHAT IS WRONG?
UM . . . I FORGET!

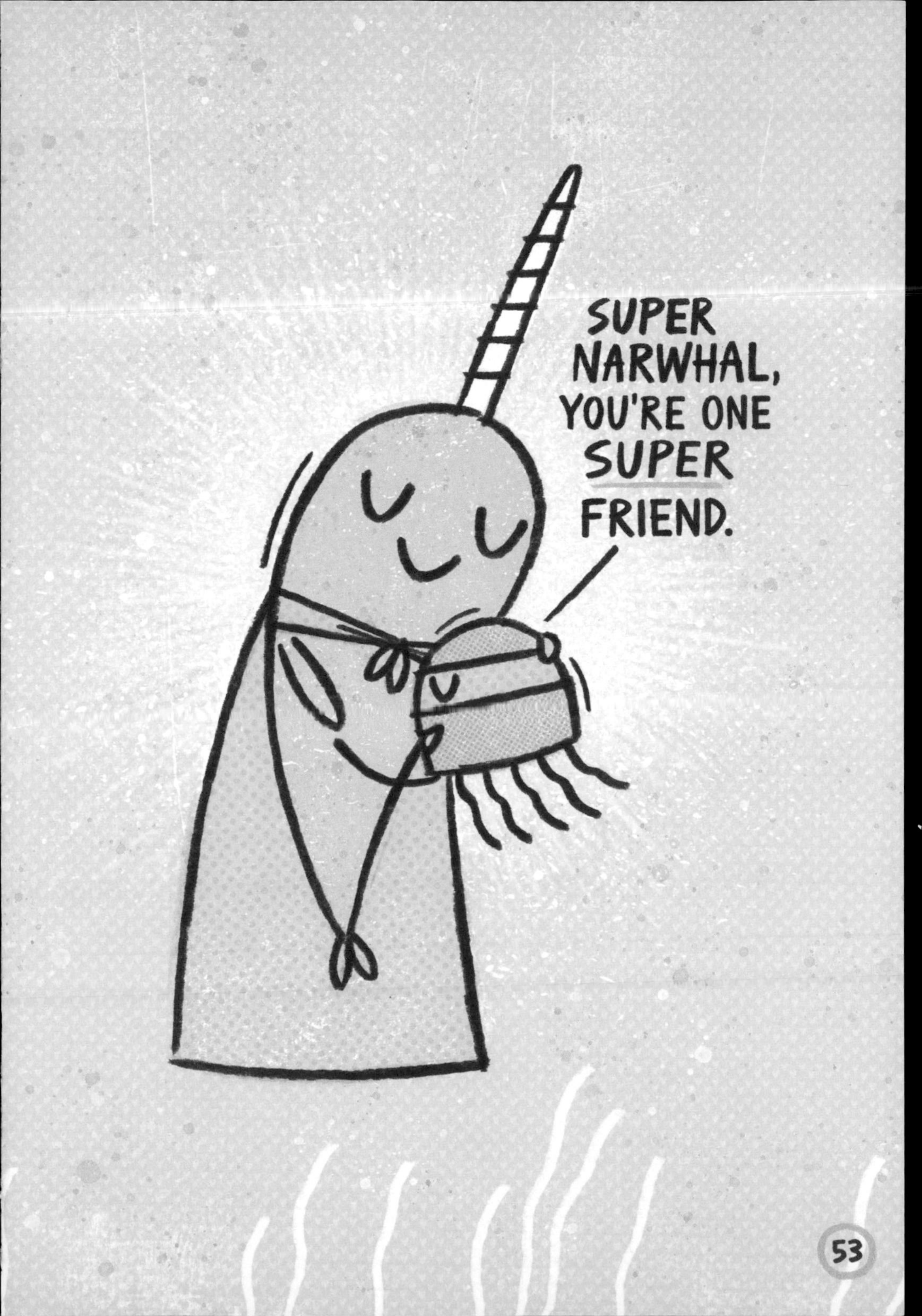
SUPER NARWHAL, YOU'RE ONE SUPER FRIEND.

OH, WAIT, NOW I REMEMBER...

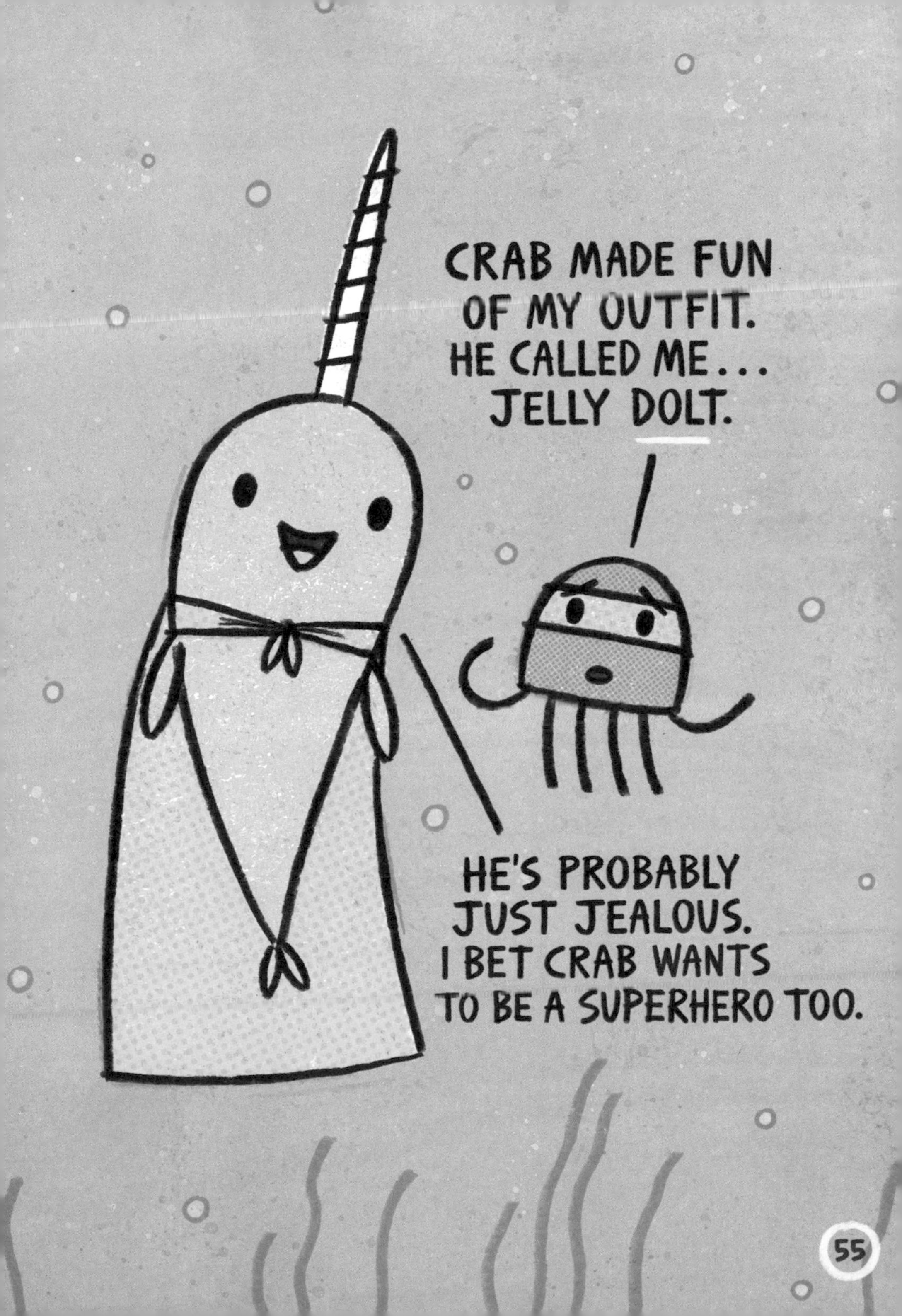
CRAB MADE FUN OF MY OUTFIT. HE CALLED ME... JELLY DOLT.
HE'S PROBABLY JUST JEALOUS. I BET CRAB WANTS TO BE A SUPERHERO TOO.

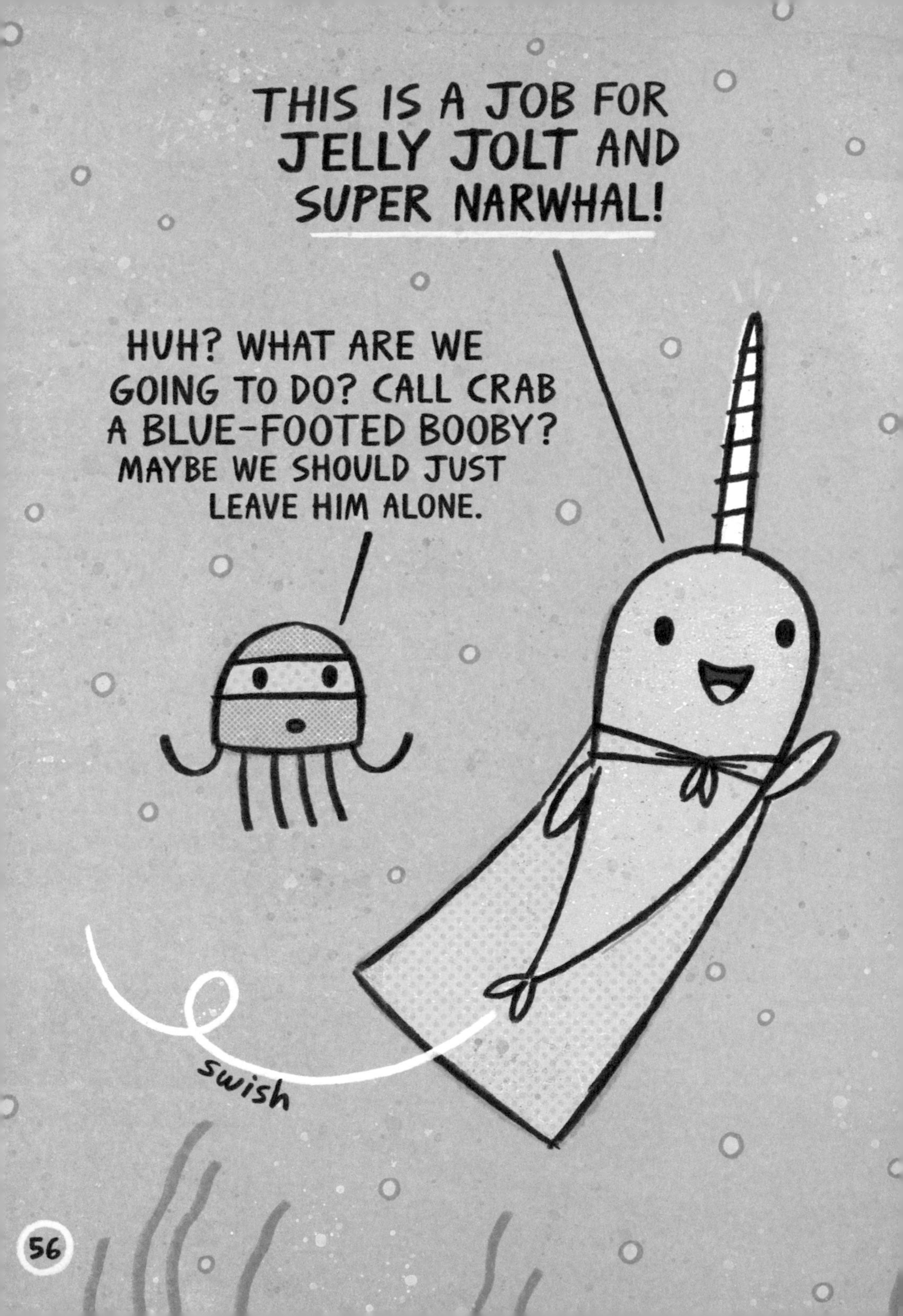
THIS IS A JOB FOR JELLY JOLT AND SUPER NARWHAL!
HUH? WHAT ARE WE GOING TO DO? CALL CRAB A BLUE-FOOTED BOOBY? MAYBE WE SHOULD JUST LEAVE HIM ALONE.
swish

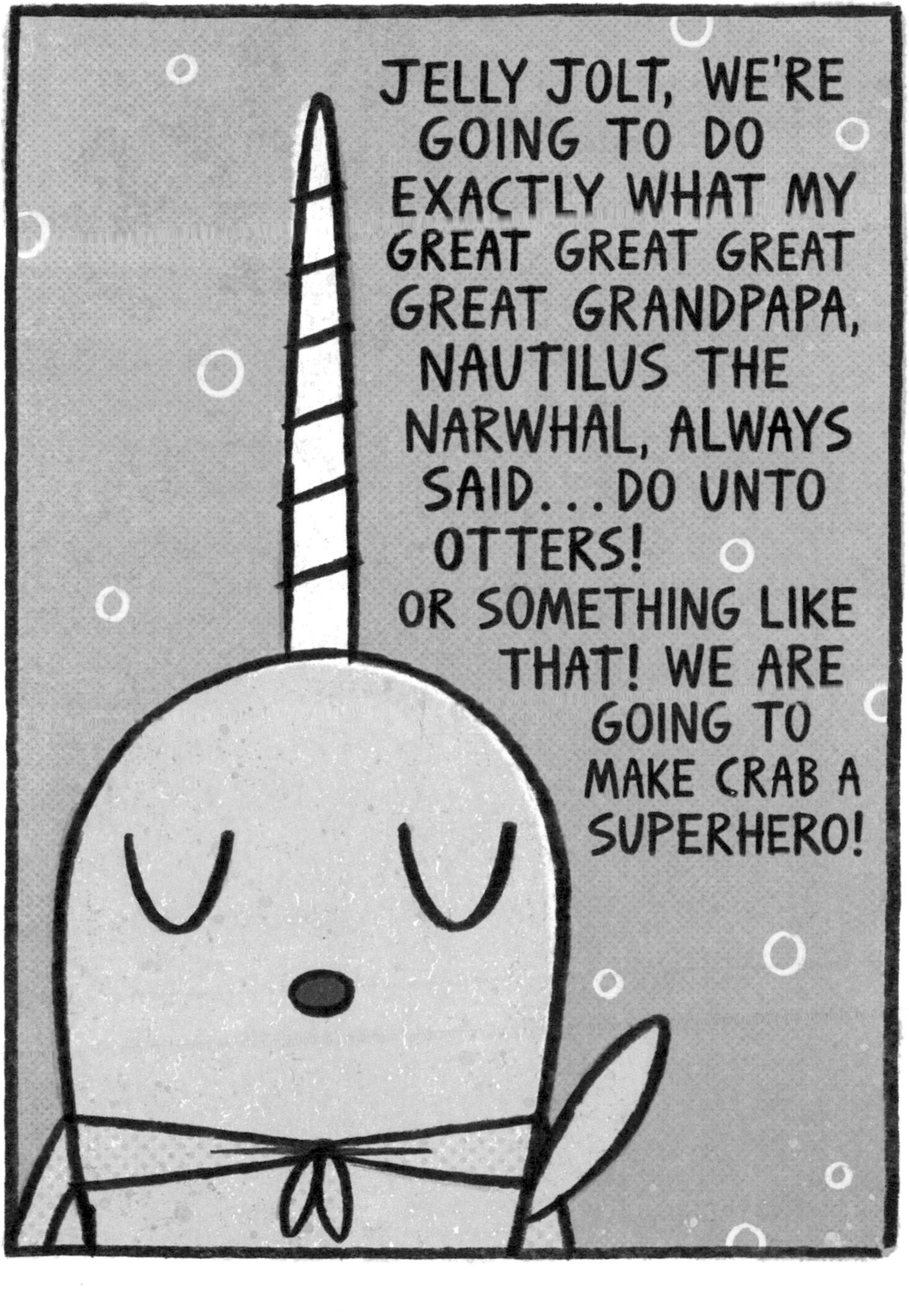
JELLY JOLT, WE'RE GOING TO DO EXACTLY WHAT MY GREAT GREAT GREAT GREAT GRANDPAPA, NAUTILUS THE NARWHAL, ALWAYS SAID...DO UNTO OTTERS!
OR SOMETHING LIKE THAT! WE ARE GOING TO MAKE CRAB A SUPERHERO!

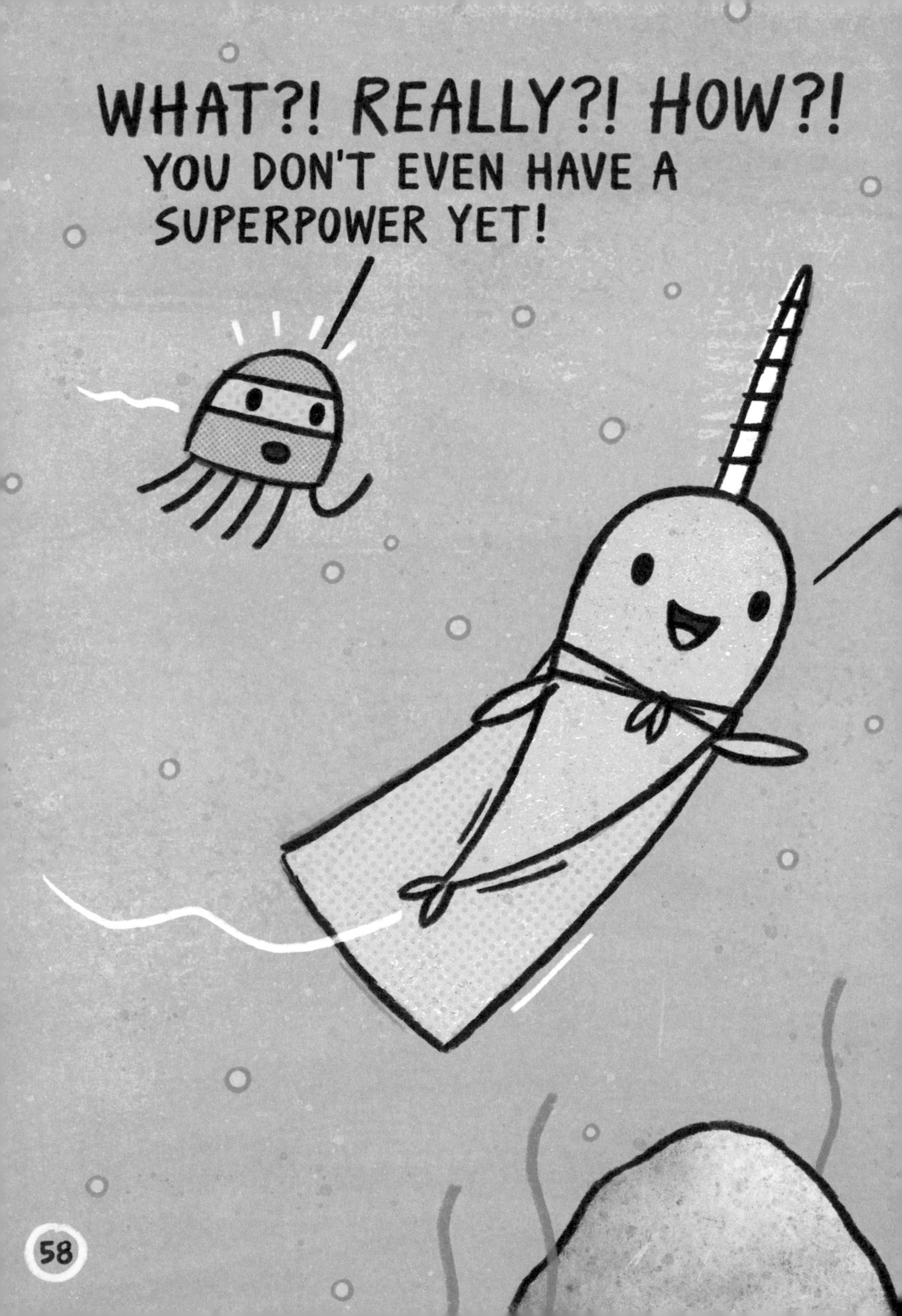
WHAT?! REALLY?! HOW?! YOU DON'T EVEN HAVE A SUPERPOWER YET!

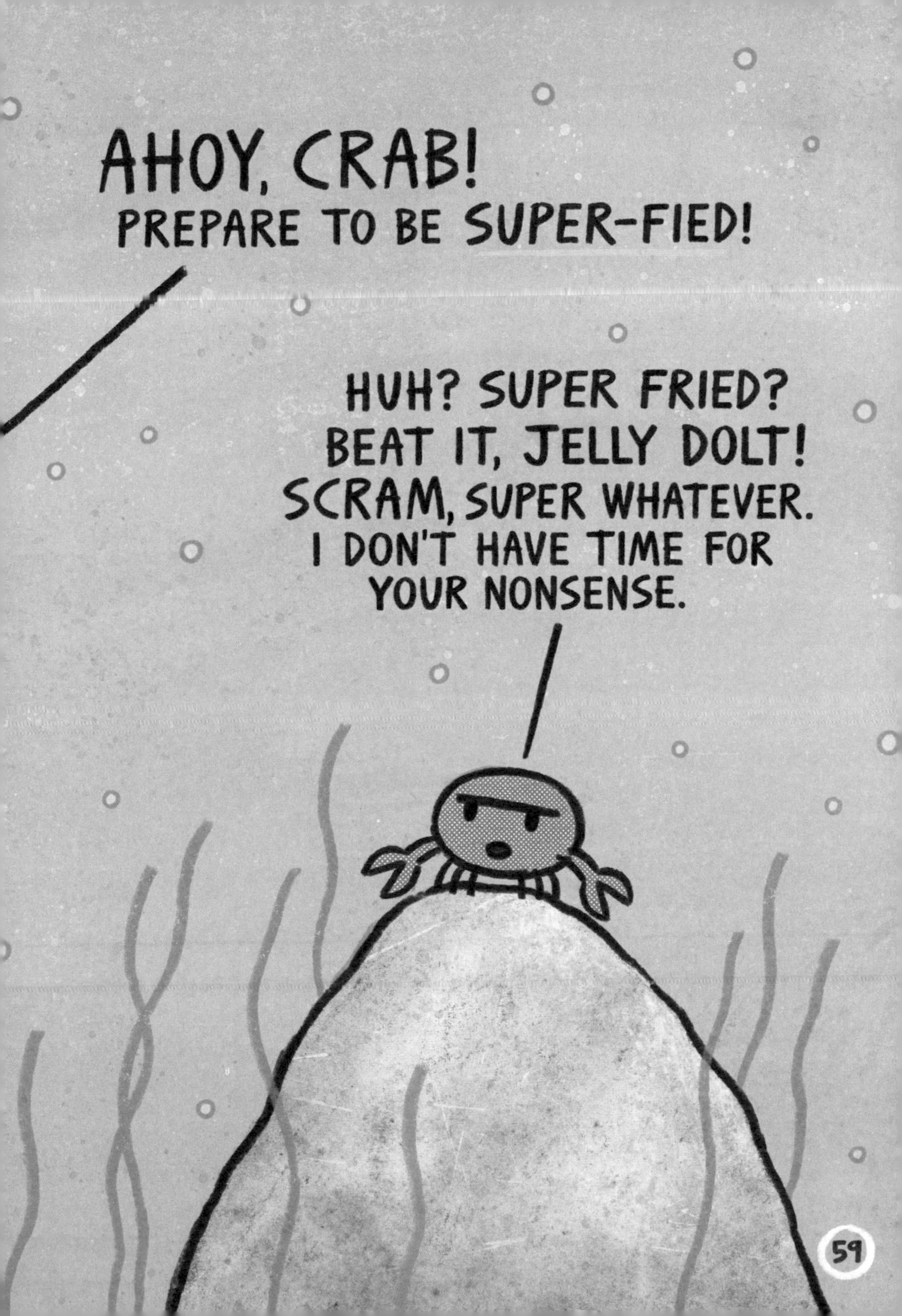
AHOY, CRAB! PREPARE TO BE SUPER-FIED!
HUH? SUPER FRIED? BEAT IT, JELLY DOLT! SCRAM, SUPER WHATEVER. I DON'T HAVE TIME FOR YOUR NONSENSE.

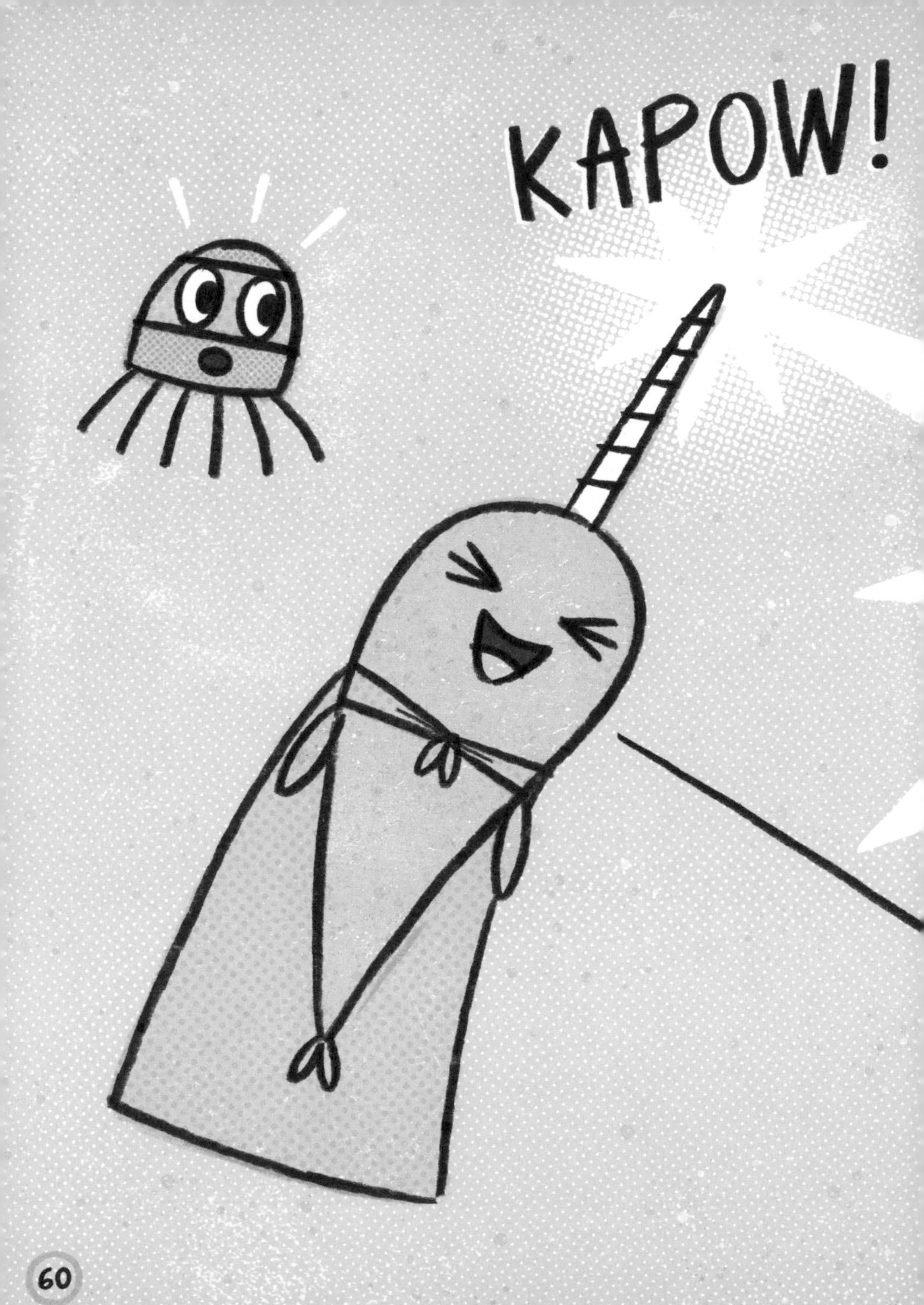
KAPOW!

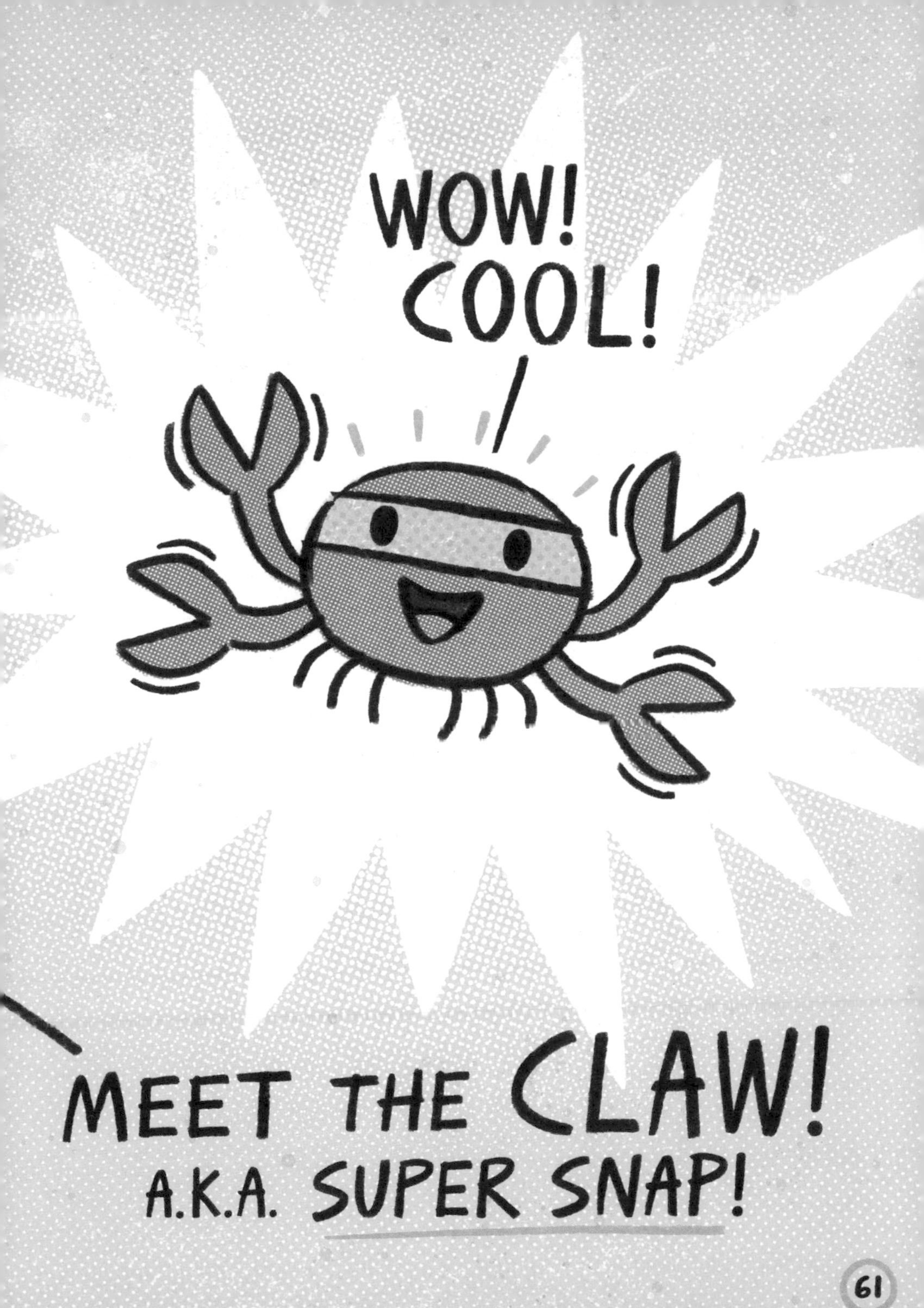
WOW! COOL!
MEET THE CLAW!
A.K.A. SUPER SNAP!

WHOA! I CAN'T BELIEVE IT! YOUR SUPERPOWER IS THE POWER TO BRING OUT THE SUPER IN OTHERS!

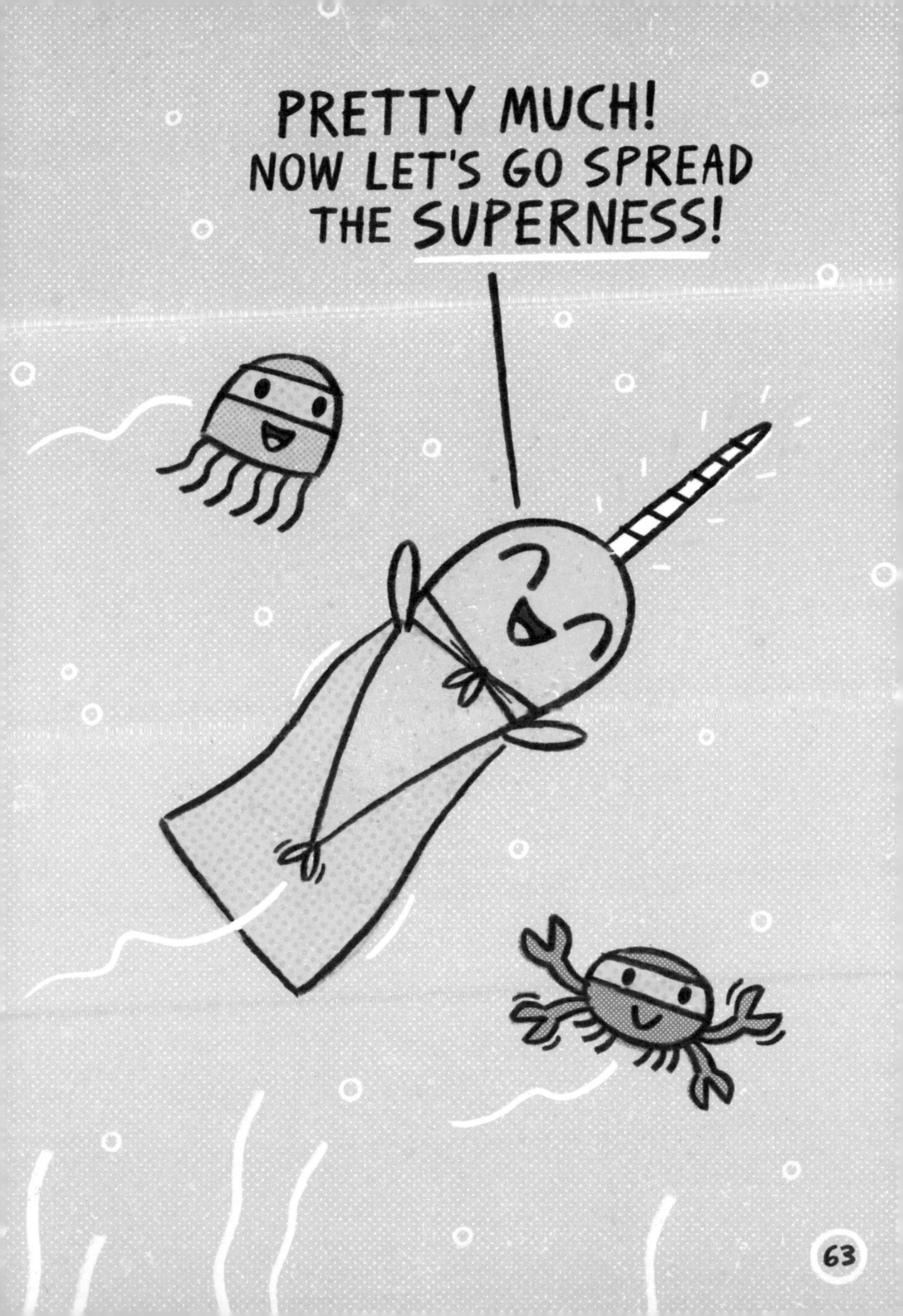
PRETTY MUCH!
NOW LET'S GO SPREAD THE SUPERNESS!

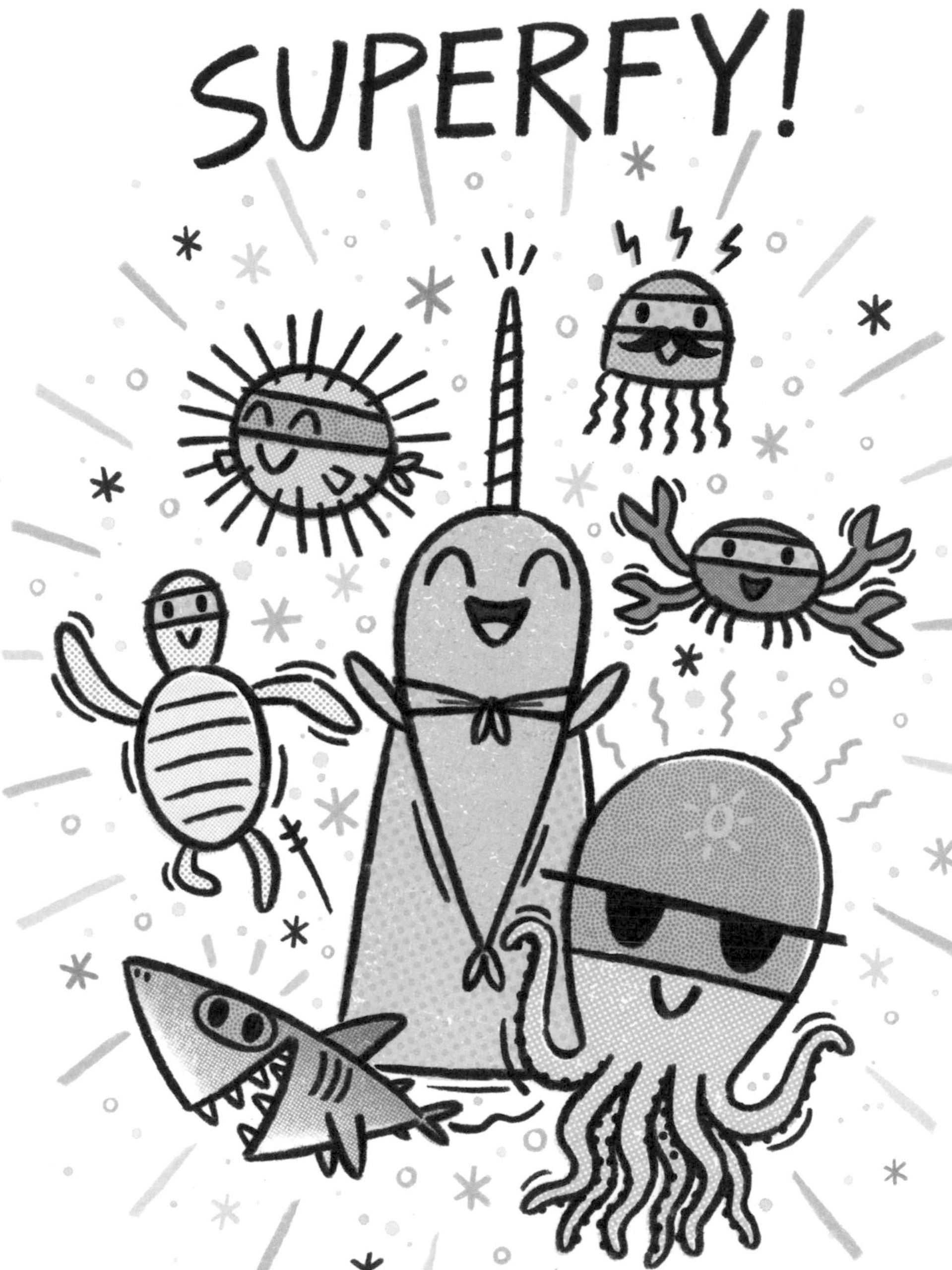
SUPERFY!